I0726625

Ecclesia.

Ecclesia.

/grieve chronic\

Angel Brynner

KoKoPelliMa Press

MIAMI   NEW ORLEANS
KOKOPELLIMAPRESS.COM

Library of Congress
Cataloguing- in- Publication Data Brynner, Angel
Elysum, grievechronic/ Angel Brynner

Audiobook edition
ISBN: 978-1-950077-26-7
Copyright © 2026 Angel Brynner

Third edition
ISBN: 978-1-950077-75-5
Library of Congress Control Number: 2014958917

First edition
ISBN:978-0-9911531-2-1
Copyright © 2003 Angel Brynner

Cover and book design by AOLAB. Additional artwork credit:
MACROVECTOR/FREEPIK, 4045/FREEPIK | FREEPIK AI

To your knees.
Ecclesia.

System down.
By all means necessary.

Ecclesia.

For Love.

...For my underground comrades in arms.

*...and for the pockets of holiness found behind and
beneath the battlegrounds of all profane worlds.*

chapter one

Kahn left the Others lounging in front of the huge video scrims that lined the wall around the bamboo garden. They cleaned themselves, sprawled like gigantic tigers, sticky with the fresh blood of being patched into one another.

Some altered skeletal structures while others only went as far as streaming new hairstyles or self-stenciling tan lines only slightly askew from what the entities had projected prior to patch-in. Some spread themselves out in a smear of colors on the floor and raised themselves up anew, fully outfitted in laser-cut layers of leather. A few worked more piecemeal, an incised brow here, sprinkled with shards of diamonds. They looked like the universe personified within the confines of a room, the chaos of the heavens in control inexplicably across their energies.

One at a time the Others beamed up into the lights above the Anjuge's bacchanal, preparing to dive. It was like observing a mini-universe of mankind, a giant pocket watch they had collectively created as an anti-Empyrean outpost.

In strobe-lit flashes the Awares took over the pedestals of the club from the night's performers, pushing the paids off into the crowd as synchronized limbs sliced through the air in time to the Lords of Acid weaving its way back into Tengu's mix. As Artyo and the ones who had gone devic alongside her whirled around counterclockwise on scattered platforms, revelers danced in the opposite direction until they were wet with sweat, screaming at the top of their lungs to the music. One by one, the Others transfigured themselves from above, beaming their spiritual bodies into the mix.

Futants and Latents bumped against the bases of speakers like they were altars. Cages made of light strobed for all to see as the Others made their way deep into the crush of bodies, hitting party-goers with the holy ghost as they passed through them. The main space filled with a swirl of deep blue light as the atmosphere became thick with expanses of stars roaring in clouds of club smoke. A red ball of fire began barreling from its spot on the edge of it all towards Earth as it began to take shape in the light show. Grown-ups in fuck me gear became little kids screaming silly things at the sky suddenly intricately tricked out above them, indoors.

"-It's Halley's comet!!"
"That's a planet-that's a friggin planet-Pluto!!! That-"
"Pluto isn't red-it's Mars-No!! Vulcan-Planet X!"
The Others looked around slyly as chaotic trumpet notes erupted out of the speaker system, causing the revelers to cover their ears and feel the pulse of the bass thru the floors until the horns wove into a trembling melody that somehow set the perimeters of the night. Kode IV exploded through the sound system.

"PEOPLE OF EARTH- ATTENTION Accelerate!....WE ARE THE SURVIVORS- OF A DISINTEGRATED SOLAR SYSTEM-"

All in attendance tilted heads to the side, raised up onto the balls of their feet by the force of it all. The Others climbed upon their altars like sacrificial kings, transporting Awares to the crowd like they were healed; lording over all, twitching to the tempo the Tengu toyed with them through. "FASTER AND FASTER-"

PEOPLE OF Earth! ATTENTION-

Angels, Futants, and Offspring began to dervish inches above platforms like spinning tops as the first scream ripped out of the Anjuge's chest in time to their Nephilimic anthem, directives cloaked in the tonalities of her screech like Morse code. Latents and posers looked on in awe as two-armed transsexuals had four in a blink of an eye.

"YOU GIVE US THREE MINUTES AND WE'LL GIVE YOU THE WORLD-

PEOPLE OF Earth! ATTENTION- ACCELERATE-"

"We are not Gods- there IS only ONE-"

The mantra spun in on itself, making its way into the hearts of everyone in attendance. Latents spun counter-clockwise around the Others as they bounced as if the music was radiating from them, imploring them to move as if grinding filthy new universes into existence. Demiurgic energies screamed to each other above the heads of revelers too high off of atmospheric intensities to write off the spiritual truths they saw staring into the gyrating trunks of the daemons hyping the crowd up until ALL were dancing as close to the rafters as these supernatural Shakers were. Fists pounded the air, backs and platforms as cries of freedom and flight exploded out of the bellies of humans whose feet left the ground as they danced, breaking chains, knowing in that sonic instant that they were as powerful as the ones swearing up and down they weren't Gods that were rallying their souls up after surviving that weeks' slaughter.

The Anjuge kept bellowing as Tengu fell into a white-hot Gospel House fit. Latents fell out and were crowd-surfed to the sidelines in droves as Awares jacked all kinds of bodies every which way to the rhythm.

"A PLANET DOOMED TO DESTRUCTION we-ACCELERATION-

we -FASTER AND FASTER-
we are the survivors of a disintegrated solar system- We are not gods-there is Only One-
WEIRD, FANTASTIC BEINGS OF A SUPER INTELLIGENCE-"

The Anjuge slipped into the mayhem that was veneration underground as Say goodbye to Love by Kenna hit the mix and the crowd went crazy. She flirtatiously messed the gigantic fall of Heian court hair that trailed behind her, primping as she strode out of the shadows like Goliath, as if the spotlight cages were protecting them from her and not the other way around. The crowd screamed for more as she laughed in the shadows of strobe lights. Then the whole place went dark. The entire club got quiet for a split second and then roared in expectation. Tengu counted off to himself in the suspended spin box and suddenly the entire place erupted with the sound of an excited heartbeat, marching and flashes. The Anjuge's roar of laughter slid out, microphones in the stage floor picking up the sound of her zebra-print, stiletto-heeled, thigh-high boots as I sit on Acid sashayed to the front of the mix. Vibrantly painted tigers attacked gazelles across the savannah that was depicted along the hem of the black- cropped kimono that swirled around the tops of her thighs. Bears swatted at salmon in rushing rivers under starry skies along its exaggerated sleeves.

The goldenrod slubbed silk of the obi was a few shades cooler than the tangerine of the painted tigers on the kimono, which made the white of Japanese script that danced across it stand out all the more. A two-inch wide wrap of African mud-cloth cut across the middle of the obi and bowed at its back. Silk ties of red, blue, and green held snugly in place across the center of the costume, the matte blood-red of the kimono's undyr loose against the gold-dusted, honeyed gleam of her exposed decolletage.

Shadows from the Anjuge's layers of eyelashes fluttered like black moths across the pearl-white geisha makeup that began about an inch below her hairline and faded out across the bones of her cheeks and under the crook of her lips. Cherry-red lids hyped the honey undertones of her skin, which had been amped-up everywhere else it was exposed. The stalking across the stage continued as her henchmen filed in behind her, decked out in variations on the same theme of reflective shades, full-body tattoos, face jewelry, fans, and fishnet stained blue and twisted around upper and lower parts of bodies at will. They glinted like dark stars, skin studded with diamond chunks. Lights continued to strobe as she seductively crouched down close to the edge of the stage, slowing down the swagger of her hips, mouth dropping open as she slid against herself pin-up girl style, back arched, face tilted up as if she was basking in the sun.

As boys and girls front and center howled, gyrating harder than ever for her attention, the Anjuge dragged her vermilion- dipped finger-tips down the windowpane fishnets that encased her thighs until they settled softly on her knees, slowly splaying her left knee out as she rocked her pelvis side to side, head thrown back as if in the throes of the god- like fornication she was effectively communicating to all as Lil Louis spun to the forefront.

"gotta tell me am i doing it right,"
"Gotta tell me am i doing it right," she purred again and again, caught up in the same throes as Tengu above, lost in the joy in repetition for all to see.

The place went crazy. Artyo cracked up as lyrics from Lil Louie's "French Kiss" began to tumble out of her mouth in time to the staccato of Tengu lube-ingthe crowd before the beginnings of the Anjuge's own Crash began to riff deep within the mix. The Others continued to spin above their appointed altars as newly christened believers got overwhelmed by the intensity of staring up at the feet of break-dancing bodhisattvas lost in their own theme songs zigzagging through the Tengu mix.

"...you thought you'd follow me and then I'd pull you thru-"

All at once the arms of Artyo, Offspring, Futants, and Angels shot overhead as they collectively began to spin, shaking to the rise and fall of the raspy voice of the Anjuge.

Too fucking lazy to do what you must do-
under this circumstance-alone I'll barrel thru ...there's nothing else to say but No, won't carry you- "

Each one danced as if going for broke, drunk off mass movement and an ability to sing along with whatever the words meant to them without any judgments. The entire environment synched up, jutting elbows and thrusting hips becoming details in a beautifully stylized orgy of ecstasy.

As the Anjuge continued to stalk around like a tiger in heat on the stage, her entourage fanned out around her like a web of stardom intent on trapping her as she sang at the top of her lungs. Suddenly they began to sing a repeat of the lyrics a beat behind her like barking dogs on the hunt, a Greek chorus careening towards the climax in the most violent Shakespearean tragedy.

Dancing across your grave- there's nothing you can do the hate you sent to me
Is overcoming you-

Posers who had gained first-time entry for the sake of appearances stepped back to avoid flailing arms and spinning bodies, only to get caught up in the torque around the holy rollers they had been trying to give pockets of space to do what came out of them without pause.

Dancing across your grave- I'm happy that you're dead-"
the hate you sent to me Is ringing in your head-

The last of the gravity disappeared and it was like no one could touch the ground even if they tried.

Dancing across your grave NO-I will not save you the hate you aimed at me Is coming back for you-

Artyo whirled around the upper bodies of people she didn't know like she was the ether surrounding them on a day to day. People danced into the personal space of one another the way energies cavorted before elements pulled apart. She wasn't in heaven; she was slicing through things that were before heaven and hell, putting universal paths into proper places according to the whims and whirls of her and the creator that had to be beyond it all, angels and demons dancing alongside her. The energy rocking the space was primordial, the return of all to what it was before the dichotomy began.

"Your blood absolved my pain-Blissed out and drenched in red-" The dancers split into three groups and grabbed the Anjuge by the arms and legs, pulling her into them like they were trying to tear her apart. Like a mountain lion surveying its most recent kill and daring anyone to approach it, she crawled over them as she roughly sang out to the crowd, the partygoers yelling the lyrics to the song back to her as they danced to the whirling bass undergirding the extravaganza and the rise and fall of the chanting voices enveloping the Anjuge.

Silently, Artyo said goodbye to Club Metropolis, one of the few places she'd felt safe in growing up in hell on Earth. She looked around at the seemingly ageless Magii who'd kept her safe in what was looked at by day-trippers as the epitome of Seoul, sentinels strutting around amongst the exiles and awols that had found their way underground like her for respite. She moved through the percolating club-kids on the platform towards the edge and eased herself down onto her knees to dismount,looking like she were about to pray.

"cause I am unashamed- and glad you all are dead-"

Out of nowhere, the Anjuge let out one of the howls she was infamous for and was launched, flying through the air directly at Artyo, flung from the stage by her crew.

Screaming like a banshee, the Anjuge violently tackled Artyo and pinned her to the platform. Artyo screamed in shock as the Anjuge grabbed her head and mercilessly rammed it into the platform floor, knocking her unconscious.

The Others looked up.

Every light in Metropolis went out as video streams from the day's earlier events and what had led to them began to pulse out silently overhead in the dark for all to see.

chapter two

Kahn made his way through the antechamber out into a corridor lined with benches on the left and flat holographic scrims strung like animal hides to the right. One end of the hall sped away into the darkness of the complex, while the other looked out onto one of the many inner rooftop levels that opened up onto the sky.

He settled down on one of the glyph-stamped suede loungers and pressed against the curved corrugated metal walls in the dark. His eyes glazed over in search of the climaxes that he knew were currently going down elsewhere, activities he knew would soon be linking up with Artyo's whether she wanted them to or not. The blurry images on the flat-screen seemed to be lunging after his thoughts.

The screen in front of him suddenly filled with static before breaking up into an off-kilter image of an ornately carved merry-go-round sitting in the middle of a patch of green grass that was edged with gnarled cypress trees and lit by headlights from cars that circled it. Kahn saw the shadows of the guardian angels originally assigned to the progeny sitting passively atop the trees that surrounded the glen and sprawled across the pinnacle of the kiddy ride. Fallen Angels-Ulteriors sat on the hoods of sport-utility vehicles, waiting. The physically regressed progeny stepped into the forefront of the screen, one by one, stating their name, age, what had been done to them and by whom, and what they had done due to it over the years, between downing handfuls of ecstasy tablets and Aleve pills chugged with bottles of Killer Kool-Aid-GHB spliced with Datura root and Angel Dust in water, cut with a Red Bull for the taurine. They were still dressed in the diaphanous GLYPH tanks, leggings and tees, now blackened and stiff with poisoned blood from the day's earlier uprising.

With each kid, the descriptions of abuse absorbed became worse, and the things they had quietly done to equalize the pain became all the more comically standard in the self-medication arena. Anger rose as voices became shrill describing overachiever burnouts erupting at age 9.12.15.18. 21.25- Whenever it registered to them that no matter how hard they worked at being the perfect kid or adult, they still weren't going to be protected from the violent insanity that underscored their days. Rampant alcoholism and frigidity after bouts of promiscuity and debauchery did little to numb out inner turmoil over past insurrections. Abusively toxic relationships in both directions kept any successes weighed down. Violence, drug use, work addictions, depression, diabetes, food issues. They didn't sound like children under the age of 18 that they now looked like, but like bitter old men and women who had lived through battles and returned from war, only to be ostracized by the blood they had to spill in order to survive.

As the Molotov cocktails hit their bloodstream and the childlike energies buried deep within them began to explode out all the more in torrents of impatience and activity, they cracked up at seeing light in the each other's eyes that hadn't been seen in ages. They cried out happily, seeing spirits they had thought died long ago, joy erupting as protective dental dams got spat out mid-hugs to one another in giddy spurts for the last times in their lives. They began to playfully push and shove each other out of the way of the camera to add on to their eulogies. Shout-outs to childhood friends who had gone through and died due to similar things in solitude bubbled up between crying, laughing, and nodding jags as their shape-shifted bodies physically relived the pre-meditated attacks on their parents due to the crossing of the GHB with the high-grade heroin in the x.

"This is on behalf of all the kids out there you let this happen to -" One cousin jeered into the screen. "You think other kids out there won't know what really happened?" Playful punches flew.

"-No matter how you adults try to suppress-suppress it-spin this on your 24 hour coverage... they'll know-" another called out as she was shoved out the way.

"You think they won't mimic us- see how ineffective all else is against what you all set us up for in comparison?!"

"Come on!! -This is a 45 minute memory stick-hurry the fuck up- you've had your turn- move!"

"You'll make us media monsters for slaying the real ones we begged you to protect us from-" pitched in a boy as two of his older female cousins knocked him away from the camera.

"This" slurred Nixa,"-is self-help at its finest!" She giggled as she spun around due to the way the x made the wind feel on her face. She slammed into her cousin and began to heave. One began to throw punches at Nixa's down-turned head. A handful of cousins swarmed on Nixa and dragged her bloodied body back towards the merry-go-round.

"You set us up to shut us -shut us down," screamed another

cousin at the top of her lungs, both eyes bloodied, instinctively veering to the left to avoid toppling the camera.

"You looked the other way when your grown friend decided he "knew me in another life-"

"Because no one protected you, you don't protect your own kids-"

"You do nothing to stop your friends from doing things to them-" ranted another.

"Your daughter isn't "FAST!" She's fucking nine years old, you sick, lazy fuck-!"

"Why would you believe the person she told you did things to her before her? Lying on good old so and so! He wouldn't hurt a -?! It's crazy!"

"Kids shouldn't even be able to describe this shit-They were making it up?! You perverted adults flooding the airwaves with sexualized children and perversions so you can have your loophole out - she seduced me?! She's six! You're all psychos!"

The roughhousing got more violent as the diatribes continued, spat out so they could be left in the realm they had gone down in.

"How many daughters got attacked by their mothers out of jealousy over scum they should have never had near their kids in the first place-?!"

"How many more guys ended up gay trying to fight off the shame of what their older brothers and sisters, or worse yet what their own parents, grandparents, uncles and aunts- did to them as children?"

"You were not born that way!!! They did that to you, son! They raped you! Then told you that you felt something, or started it-that you must have liked it and had been that way from the beginning- they put the guilt on you at age four! That's why you're fucked up!"

"How many more size six women are wasting away inside of size 22 bodies, eating themselves to death, insulated against anybody ever "getting at" them again?!"

Maniacal laughter exploded somewhere in the background as the progeny began to chase each other around the merry-go- round, tackling each other to the ground and hitting whoever fell first until they stopped breathing, then turning on the next nearest to the ground to offer them up.

Behind the bloodied insane adolescents being dragged back towards the merry-go-round, leaves on cypress trees rustled with the cries of aghast guardian angels taking it all in. One by one they fell from the trees, only to be pulled back

skyward, strung up by the chains of Empyrean counsel that had been fastened around their necks the entire time, lynching them and leaving them for lost in the trees. They were coated with blood as it drained out of the ones they'd been assigned to, screaming like thorn birds as they took in what these kids were driven to do to free themselves from their impotent watch.

Ulterior Rogues in divisions synched up under Kahn and the Others sat on the hoods of the repossessed parental SUVs, hoping for it all to end soon, watching the sky as the immolation vibrated up through the cosmos, Ancients bearing witness and sanctifying the scarred and chipped young adults as they beat one another to the brink of delicate new births.

Agonized guardian angels hung upside-down in trees, spiritually slaughtered by the treasons committed that they now felt deep within. Their angelic howls exploded scales off of their own angelic earlobes, cut to the quick by the their charges as they wailed through beating one another to death. The guardians began to cry out allegiance to the Ulteriors as the only way the blood coating them could ever be washed off.

"And you have no excuse!" A boy cousin screamed as an elbow knocked him down in front of the camera. More cousins entered the fray, punching until fists were red with blood and nails were thick with gore from ripping through skin. "You let us all know how worthless we were to you-" he squealed before he got kicked in the mouth.

"You think getting old is going to save you? Stop it from coming back to make you pay for what you did?! You're a senior citizen now? I was five, you asshole! Five! Alzheimer's my ass! If all of us have to rise up against you to make you recall, we will!" A punch landed on his jaw and he spat out a tooth that bounced off the lens. Aghast guardians moaned, coated in gore behind it all, unable to stop the suicidal violence as it erupted before them. The progeny dropped like psychotic flies in the final moments of their last day.

"Why would I want to bond with you over "it happened to you too?" You still would not do anything to make it stop! Why wouldn't that make you help more?" squealed another who picked up the thread as her cousin died in her arms.

"You called this Armageddon on yourselves!" He choked as life left him.

"Bust the fuck who raped your niece!- Lock up those who covered it up, instead of looking for evidence to lock me up in juvie to shut me up!"

Arms reached up from below and took another one down closer to the front as they all crawled back towards the carved horses like privates crawling through enemy territory towards safety.

"Do your job! Parents, DO your job- protect Us!" wheezed Maria, the last cousin standing.

"Protect the generation you plan on having wipe your baby boomer asses as senility tries to set in over the twisted shit you did-" she heaved, "...so you can pretend like you don't remember-"

Maria slowly looked around at the remains of her own generation. Bloodied children and emancipated teenagers crawled towards the merry-go-round to join the ones who had already made their way to it, dragging the corpses of those who'd had the life beaten out of them in the grass before it. Streaks of red complemented the green of grass that had somehow survived a brutal summer. She could now see lynched guardian angels dangling from trees, missions violently aborted, absorbing the spilt blood of their charges in the background.

"When you get tired of having no voice-get emptied of all hope for the life you came down here to-have - finally let it kill you-" Maria whispered, unable to feel her tongue or the pain from cracked ribs due to the bliss of the cocktail of drugs coasting through her broken body.

"–With nothing left to defend- or fear-" she spat self-consciously, momentarily losing her last train of thought.

The tide of internal bleeding crested in the whites of her eyes as she stared lucidly into the camera and began to slide slowly down her cheeks like tears of blood.

With a fluttery flip of the zoom switch, Maria re-focused the camera lens. She turned and began to limp towards the merry-go-round.

"You've shown us...that the only thing that will stop you from devouring us-" she sputtered over her shoulder, "-is for those whose childhoods you cannibalized to attack back en masse. It's us against you now."

She got to the control box of the merry-go-round and pulled down the lever. Maria slumped down amongst the progeny as the merry-go-round whirled into motion.

"Your Sexual Revolution has slaughtered us all." she whispered, then died.

The memory stick ran out watching the last of the progeny die, arms wrapped around one another as sporadic spurts of laughter and slobber slipped out of their dying bodies.

chapter three

Kahn slumped in front of the screen as the massacre slammed into him. When the last of the progeny passed away, the wails of their guardian angels stopped.

One by one, the Ulteriors released the angels from their Empyrean-engineered snares so they could officially fall. The spiritual kindred looked into one another, blood-stained parts of them finally understanding things that had gone down so long ago. Dressed only in the giveaway red, green and blue, the Ulteriors cornered the spiritually suicidal angels three on one and told them where they stood. The ulterior Apoc narrowed his pale blue eyes under thick black brows as he murmured in the bleeding earlobe of one angel.

"Now-you can abide by consular edict and not escort these children- these killers into the highest high-" he flicked a strand of bloody gunk off the sleeve of his bespoke suit cut from sashiko-quilted indigo fabric.

"...And move through all realms from this point onward soaked with their blood," Apogee deadpanned, dragging her blood-soaked hands through the beautiful blond hair of the fallen angel under press by them. Her brazil nut toned skin gleamed as if lacquered in blood in some spots. Her red pinstriped pants were marred by bloody palm-prints that seeped through the fibers and scarred her numb skin. Even her Mohawk had clumps of gore in it. Her red belly muscle tank was one of the few places that hadn't been stained as they brought the new recruits down.

"Their sacrificial blood will be all that is sensed on your now fallen angel asses from this point onward-" Growled

Apex. He looked down at the bloodied green grass swishing between his exposed toes to stop from shoving the newly fallen back into the tree they'd just pulled him down from for having let it come to this. "...OR... give your charges the cloaked passage -alongside you -into the Empyrean- that they deserve. Since you had the option of helping the whole time but did not." The hems of Apex's green silk shantung drawstring pants were flecked with blood and broken bits of grass.

Three on one, Ulteriors instructed their newest recruits carefully. Sprinkled imperceptibly through the lines, they would tell the 13 gatekeepers the truth...that the charge had been involved in a massacre. One by one, sliding them in before the system would connect them to the particular carnage and petition for blockage. One by one, the guardian angels swooped down and picked their charges out of the crush. They tucked the souls of each passed progeny onto their respective backs before shooting up into the sky, leaving the husk-like corpses to the heat and slick red that coated the scene.

As the remaining strands of offspring exteriorly bound to him penetrated the gates of the Empyrean abode, Kahn dragged his suddenly gnarled hand through his hair. Feather-light clumps of it came out between his fingertips and slid down into his palm before dissolving into dust. Accusations Kahn hadn't thought about in eons crested in his ears.

"Leaving only Artyo's crossing." Apoc whispered, suddenly beside him, prostrate.

"Why are you- Get off your knees, Apoc- all that is-" Kahn snapped at him, absently aggravated by the pomp and circumstance of the Ulterior Angels materializing all around him.

"Look Kahn... now more than ever it's time for you to embrace the point to all this that you are-" Apogee began.

Apex continued. "Or she's not going to make it out behind you-"

"Because face it-none of the Others in positions to assist her in your absence-will step up to the plate- If you won't-" Apoc rambled on.

Riled under the glare of the Ulteriors looking to him to be led, Kahn sighed. "They'll help her in ways you all can't even fathom, for reasons you're not ready to comprehend-"

"Yes-Entities we can't even imagine will help," Apogee whispered, touching Kahn on the arm to calm him. "But out of allegiance to you, nothing else."

"You- you really need to accept this- and do what has to be done to ensure they see whose she truly is, no matter what she has done!" Apex barked.

"And that she is inadvertently who helped to initially free-" Kahn started, dropping his head as he understood, a soft smile tugging at the corners of his mouth and eyes.

"Look..." Apogee whispered hoarsely, motioning to the holoscreen Kahn had watched them on. The screen began to fill with static.

Lingering Ulteriors transfigured themselves into the hall alongside Kahn split seconds before the arrival of the energies that had the atmosphere so out of whack. The holoscreen was suddenly stuffed to capacity with beings other than those Kahn had expected, their presence spreading to activate every scrim hung along the corrugated wall of the hallway, weaponry unsheathed, arched in the air to slice through the skin of the dragons they were there to kill.

"What the fuck is that-?" Apoc hissed.

The mouths of this horde of things ripped open, the blistering air in front of them waving like 120 degree heat off asphalt. Fleshy,bruised mouths revealed row after row of perfect teeth, some blackened, some optic white, caught up in muted out howls of laughter. Sparks shot from eyes under brows that slashed away aggressively. Skins of every shade seemed metallic. Their bodies contorted in slow-motion and seemed to freeze-frame in response to the solidification of each newly materialized member of what could only be described as their hunting party.
They were obscenely aesthetic, peacock-like. Shadows from exaggerated lashes danced across their cheeks when they blinked. Tufts of hair floated in silky sheets around their heads or looked like wool just shorn from sheep, thick in the air of the blood-soaked clearing. Birds, dragons and snakes were etched in matte ochre across foreheads that gleamed as if they housed the sun. Facial hair painstakingly stenciled on vibrated as tiny globules of liquid color raced after faces that had left them suspended in the air as they silently shook with morbid laughter, waiting for whatever they were there to fight to appear.

"Whatever they are- it's an Army of 'em-"Apex coughed.

Ulteriors crowded around Kahn, staring at what had to be gods, their bodies bound up like nothing the all- spectrum sighted Ulteriors had ever seen. Retinas ached as they raced over folds of what had to be fabric woven from the blackened fronds of palm trees. Torsos were covered in what looked like tufts of cotton pressed between spider webs and stained with soot. Holsters. Corsets. Leathers festooned with chrome plated porcupine quills wrapped around legs, arms. Quills even stuck out of the skin of some of them. Coils of copper glinted as they moved counter-clockwise continually on fingers. Metal seemed to shape shift around each of them like exoskeletons folding in and out as if filled with the life-force of whomever must have died to create such magnificent pieces, waiting for their hosts to regain composure so they could clamp down into them once again. Fingertips and toes had been dipped in latex, reds, blacks, hands and feet stenciled with cryptograms in matching red, green and blue pigments.

"Hopefully one that is on our side," Apogee whispered. As if somehow suddenly aware of being watched, the cloud of Gods shifted their collective menacing gaze and peered in at the Ulteriors crowded around Kahn in the hallway.

"What the fuck-" the Ulteriors choked in unison and backed away from the entities' awareness of their presence from within the holoscreens, a presence which rarely registered to any entity on any level. The leader of the hunting party watched Kahn and his Ulteriors without blinking, hidden within the crush of the Androgynes who had originally come down to Earth from Heaven. Nefilim, loosed. She cased the band of rogue Angels with ulterior motives and the original Other like a predator, the only brow She had arched mischievously over Her left eye, tipped with a bluish-green to match the swirling shades of the pressed lapis and malachite monocle floating in front of Her eye on a thin copper chain that crawled up Her back and over Her ear like a sniper's site.

Her legs were encased with snugly cut leather chaps that had been fully embossed with a pattern resembling the weave of antique birdcages found in the caves of Hokkaido. The length of the pants were exaggerated with the excess fabric crumpling around copper-dipped toes that peaked out from the bottom of them, matching the copper hoops that crawled up Her left ear.

Her undyr was no more than a thong stained with boar's blood, a talisman. Her long black hair had been bound off of Her face in two piles like horns by silk ribbon that had been wrapped and wound tightly from the edges of Her high forehead back for about half a yard, ribbon dyed in the blood of sacrificed boars, the cloaked birthright of that from which She'd originally sprung. In the center of Her glowing forehead was a neatly etched spider in red ochre. A thick smear of liquefied copper was spread across Her breasts.

Gauze the color of Her skin wound around Her waist, only perceptible due to its lack of iridescence and the splattered blood of the progeny on it as She dragged Her bloodied hand absently across herself. Sitting even lower on Her hips than the waistband of the chaps was an A-lined micro-mini cut from the fur of a female wolf, the side hems dipped in the same boar's blood as the ribbon that sheathed Her hair and her thong. The outyr that She was supposed to wear at all times was draped over her shoulders, pelts of porcupines whose quill tips had been dipped in chrome prior to sacrifice, sewn together for Her with strands of fiberglass. The only glyphs on Her skin were the boar's blood birthright blessing incised into the small of her back, hidden under the gauze from all.

The Nefilim shifted and She floated to the forefront of the screen, legs spread in the wide relaxed stance of a cowboy, head cocked casually to the side as she sniffed the air, staring directly into them, smiling like a cat right before the kill.

Kahn's mouth dropped open. The Androgynes behind her let out a violent barrage of whistles and howls of laughter as She slowly raised Her left hand and pointed at Kahn, brought the fingers back to her lips and blew a kiss at him. Drops of the red lacquer coating them atomized off Her lips and sliced through the screen. The red splattered on his chest in the hallway and glowed in the dark like iridescent blood. The Ulteriors around him gasped at the reality of him being marked. She clicked her tongue across the side of her teeth as She sucked on them in time to a flirtatious wink of her eye. Kahn ran his hand through his hair, looking down at his chest, embarrassed for reasons he couldn't explain if he had to.

Bewildered, Apoc, Apogee and Apex raised their hands to touch the pulsating droplets of red on the chest of Kahn, stopping mid-reach as they felt Her eyes cut towards them. Red lacquer leapt off of him and onto the extended fingertips of all three of them, marking them too. Suddenly, thunder boomed overhead.

The heads of the Androgynic Nefilim Collective whipped

up towards the sky as She chuckled to herself and raised her brow as she pulled a glyph-incised katana out from its resting place between the blades of her back, letting the suddenly flickering light play off of it.

She sweetly smiled at the Ulteriors transfixed by Her presence onscreen, lips literally lacquered with the blood of Ancients silently mouthing words to her posse that the Ulteriors couldn't comprehend. On cue, streaks of color and cryptograms pushed into the skin of Her cohorts as they bled into the shadows of storm clouds passing overhead, veiled en masse.

Explosions of static-filled thunder announced the arrival of the Punishers-Narcs sent to collect data on the bloodied progeny crossing over one at a time above. She and Her clan waited in their shadows until all of the batch arrived and dismantled. The Punishers pulled the tubes out of their mouths that ensured inhalation safety between realms, black curls of carbon dioxide drizzling into the atmosphere as they took in the scene in horror. As the first Punisher went to patch into the Empyrean Sector to report the carnage below to above, the glyph scarred blade of Her katana sliced through his heavenly vocal cords as she materialized directly behind him, blooming up from his own shadow. The Androgynes swarmed on the Narcs, blades slashing out at the Punishers from within their own shadows in ambush.

Weaponry cut through spiritual bodies, spilt blood glowed as if liquefied rubies, coating the crazed beings in sacred gore as the Punishers went spasmodic before bursting into shards of black-light and smoke.

The sacre coeur coated Androgynes roared in satisfaction then cloaked themselves in shadows again in preparation for the next batch of Narcs who patched in attempting to report, buying Kahn and company time they hadn't known they needed until more blood was spilled.

The Ulteriors pressed into the walls of the hallway in complete shock by what they had just witnessed.

Shaken, Kahn stood up and walked down the hall until he was outside on one of the lower level roofs of the club. His band of red, blue and green completely unnerved Ulteriors followed a few paces behind him, led by Apogee, Apoc and Apex, staring down into the tingling red that had crawled up from their fingertips,palms and arms onto their foreheads. The roar from the giant fans that kept the complex cool enveloped the sound of curses and screaming careening inside Kahn's head as Her and her clan of cohorts cut them more time for him to do his part. This thing was already in motion and he was at bat. Shaking, Kahn pushed back through the confused cloud of Ulterior Angels.

"Come on, we haven't got much time-Don't worry- they're on our side." Kahn barked and pushed back into the depths of Metropolis, immediate exit proceedings whirling around him. The Ulteriors followed in the wake of him completely owning the path they'd all somehow ended up on.

chapter four

Artyo's grievance going-away party reeled towards its climax. The crowd was going wild. The images of Artyo and the progeny offing their parents and then themselves had been beamed out overhead in the dark to sound of thrash-funk like a latter-day silent movie as its lead lay in their midst unbeknownst to them, unconscious under the Anjuge.

She let out a peal of laughter as her whited-out eyes adjusted to the shocked look on Artyo's gape-mouthed face as she came to. Artyo started to laugh nervously before she was silenced by the Anjuge's raised finger to her lips. The Anjuge bent in as if about to kiss her and dropped a quarter-sized waxed paper packet into her mouth, then held her finger back up to Artyo's lips again. She yanked Artyo up in the dark and slammed her fists into her temples before springing up and leaping backwards, landing back on the main stage. The crowd was too high to be any more confused at the floorshow than usual. Stunned, Artyo slid off the platform and into the crowd, her temples glowing red as she groggily made her way off of the main floor. The lights in Metropolis exploded back to life and the party kept going off without a hitch.

Cutting thru all sorts of private room activity she was indifferent to on her best days, Artyo didn't notice the cloaking wallpaper morph of Kahn's clothes on her as she went, from socialite to club land demimondaine. The fabric crawled across her skin of its own will, knowing what the onlookers absently longed to see, which was that all that had been beamed onto them was just a game, staged, and the girl cutting through their zones was just a gifted actress who gave so much of herself on the screen that it made their skin crawl. She made her way towards the exit closest to the Cuyahoga river, unaware of what the Others had made everyone in attendance complicit to due to cheering her storyline on, in Technicolor. She stumbled into the foyer of Kahn's zone. The now bald but still intensely browed Kahn was sprawled across a chaise at the bottom of yet another inner skylight, surrounded by pillows and curls of smoke rising from candles and incense, looking up at the reverb of the festivities still going on. He was regal, a dying, loved king beckoning her to his side with the slightest motion of his upturned hand.

The red, blue and green Ulteriors in attendance bowed as she stepped onto and over them to reach the one who had kept her alive when her guardians had openly refused to go against consular edicts of acceptable involvement. There was nothing but joy in both of their eyes as they took one another in, understanding completely what was afoot in ways neither would ever have to put words to. Kahn pressed his hand to her face as she took in his withering head the way a child looked adoringly at her most favorite doll, oblivious to it falling apart. Artyo pulled his hand from her face and peered into it as the lines still harshly chiseled into his gnarled palm reiterated what was to happen next for her.

"This is all my fault- but I'm going to fix-" Artyo started, attempting to pay her last respects, granting him both absolution and a separate peace. When all was said and done, she would be the final portion of him to return. But the rest of the words burrowed into the phlegm in her throat. "See you on the other side," she choked stupidly as she kissed his caved-in cheek.

"You should be so lucky-" he laughed and then turned ice-cold. Suddenly, the air was filled with the crackle of electricity. "Put her out!" Kahn roared with a ferocity Artyo had never seen exploding out of him. "Remove her from the premises-now!" He screeched.

Apoc yanked Artyo by the arm as Apogee dove around to her other side. Apex pulled up the rear as they slammed through the crowd of Ulteriors that jumped up wielding scythes to protect Kahn at all costs.

Artyo screamed as she struggled against being yanked away from the one who had spent his eternity protecting her through many sets of double doors. Apoc slammed his hand over her mouth and Apogee hissed at her in tongues to stay quiet as they barreled down synapse-like hall after hall. Apex charged around them, teeth and blades bared as he slammed first out onto the nearest roof. Apoc and Apogee ran up on him so hard that they all almost fell off.

Artyo went flying out over the edge to the tips of her toes and wrists in their hands, Apoc and Apogee bowing her back towards the club at the last second as Apex and Apoc violently threw Artyo and Apogee off the roof as hard as they could.

They sailed wildly through the air, landing in a controlled heap in the gutter across the street from the abandoned factory that the Metropolis complex was housed in.

"Run!!!!" Apogee hissed to a stunned Artyo, bounding

backwards up onto the roof with the re-directed force of their impact onto the ground.

An explosion erupted deep in the heart of the complex as Apex, Apoc and Apogee charged back in and doors slammed shut between them and Artyo.

Over her shoulder, pale green light pulsed into the night sky around the edges of blacked out windows before the area was suddenly drenched in a silence that made Artyo trip over her own feet as she ran like death was on her heels. The blare of the foghorn exploded as she dashed for the barge going across the lake to the farthest point east - Buffalo.

chapter five

At the bottom of the gangway, a last package from Kahn was waiting for her.

The scraggly merchant marines were so used to club-kids buying passage that she was completely ignored after fishing out the fold of bills Kahn had shoved in the bundle for the Seafarers.

The clouds held back torrents of rain destined to descend upon Cleveland until the barge had made its way out past Erie, Ohio. She looked back once at the rumbling of thunder two hours into the trip. The water near the city flickered as if the lake was on fire.

Artyo didn't flinch at the analogy. She had run out of the gates of her childhood hell and knew it. She turned towards where the sun would rise. Future memories of her route back to her true home lit up in her eyes as she sat down and gently bit into the sour skin of pomegranates packed into Kahn's care kit, settling in for the ride. She played with the packet from the Anjuge, opening it, flipping the coin in it.

The merchant marines on the barge alongside her gave Artyo the wide berth the captain had ordered. Splinters of atrocities she had both seen and done shot out of her. Heads nervously swiveled towards her as she grunted against the flashbacks that pinned her down as soon as she slid into the first layers of sleep. The stars peeking out behind strands of clouds seemed to create a frame around her slumped figure at the end of the deck. The riveted steel was cool against the back of Artyo's legs. The deeper she fell into the abyss of sleep, the more awake her spiritual body became.

In an instant, Artyo was rubbing at her eyes and taking in an old woman perched on the edge of the deck in front of her.

The old lady sat on a pillow, smiling to herself as she felt her presence register. She had a game of brightly spinning coins scattered around her on the deck that she had lost interest in long ago and was loosely shrouded in layers of tattered red, green, and blue embroidered kimonos that hung open at angles across her chest as if one had been initially slipped on after a bath, with others layered atop it in lieu of getting completely dressed. The silk seemed to pile up in the old woman's lap in never-ending twists of fabric. One leg was folded under her, the other stretched out in front at an odd angle. Her pants were a patchwork of flesh held together by millions of platinum porcupine quills whose tips had been dragged through blood Artyo could smell. The exposed skin of her chest was smeared with liquid mercury that glistened like war-paint. With every breath she took a different set of organs pushed out against her skin in bas-relief.

She looked like a graying spiral-haired child playing dress up in her mother's clothes. Obscenely long acid white ringlets hung in strategically strewn clumps around her wizened brazil-nut shaped eyes. The curls loosened, draping down over the edge of the barge and out across the expanse of water beyond her to the horizon line like veins of white- out pressed so harshly against the atmosphere that they had bunched up in places like clouds. About two inches of bare skin was visible above the red lacquer that coated her toes as if her feet had walked through it. She tilted her head towards her left shoulder as if zooming into every detail of Artyo. Artyo felt her skin twitch with her own pulse, frozen for a second by the suddenly graphic imagery of all types of cells flowing in different directions across and under her skin that flashed out of eyes that were only white. Artyo stared back at the old woman as if she were the embodiment of pornography itself, in the purest sense of the word Artyo had ever visually experienced.

"Do you actually believe... you will get away with all this?" The old woman whispered.

"You tell me, old woman-"

"I've allowed you to...to satiate your base appetite for violence and destruction-In hopes of averting the cataclysm you will set off if you are allowed to go on. But do you believe you have gotten away with this already?" The crone's black brows were elongated and incised as if mauled by a bear cub. They stood out against the honeyed color of her skin and the bright white of the hair framing her face.

"Only Fate knows if I believe I will be successful." Artyo sneered.

"Fate has no fear of you, child!" the old woman chuckled. "Then why are You here?" Artyo mocked her.

"Come now! Do you really believe you will free enough of you to truly break loose?" the old woman snorted. The fine white strands that framed her face did double-helixes around it. The woman's face brought to mind old Asian ladies permanently tanned from years of working in sun-soaked rice paddies.

"You, my child, are aiming in the wrong direction-blame ye gods, Free Will, even, but not Fate-"

"Fate can't stop me from canceling out the carnage she gives the gods license to carry out!" Artyo hissed like a viper.

"Your kind is too young to handle the-too hot-headed-with no sense of story- of backstory-of your history- what you are simply called into existence to complete-" the old woman murmured.

"You allow them to destroy us ahead of time-"
"You seem to think this is about sacrifice-
"Of course it is! You've killed off generations of us! And for what?!" Artyo roared.

"I have done No such thing- Variations of your own kind-You know not of what you speak-" the old lady snarled, slightly startled.

"You care not what you do-" Artyo seethed back. "Do not argue against the ways of the world, child!"

"It is time for your reign in this world to end, crone-Eventually...people look Up. Higher than you. That eventuality is now." Artyo snapped.

The old lady stopped mid-retort, as if the concept of anything higher than her was so far gone in the abyss of her memory that it threw her for a loop. But she was too far removed from the storylines she had spinning like the tiny coins around her to have any sympathy for little more than the equivalent of an extra attempting to rewrite a role to stay gone for long. "Nevertheless, there is no way you will be able to get through. Do not waste an old mother's time nor try her patience- " the lady cooed.

"Two aspects of me have already crossed, crone," Artyo snarled, interrupting her.

"You? -Against me? No ONE will help you! No One! You do not comprehend what I am! The Necessity of-" The old woman snapped then changed tracks. "Your inner gate-keepers were broken long ago just to ensure your failure at a time such as this- they have never been allowed to grow – like they can escape?" the old lady purred.

"Oh- you have to be grown to get out? Thanks for that tidbit- I didn't know that." Artyo smiled sweetly.

The old woman narrowed her eyes, then gave the most pornographically plastic smile . "You can't take the pain it'd take to even wake them from my-"

"I've taken the pain of all else you've done without going out of my mind-" Artyo smirked.

"Says the woman-child who just killed not one but two generations of her own family with one tiny decision.. .you're all alone-" the old lady sniffed.

"And yet even You are Here to try and talk me out of this. Out of necessity, of course-"

"See! This is why the splintering is allowed-you don't have the time to start, and you don't know where on earth to even begin." the old lady sneered. "Who in Heaven, Hell or Earth will help you now against Me?" she bellowed.

"45 that even I can see just did- never mind the hordes I supposedly can't yet always have seen, all with just as much reason to want you off your twisted throne." Artyo laughed.

"And there are legions where they came from, backed by millions we believe in even though we can't even see them yet-"

"Why would you believe that you-will live to see anything else beyond this sinking ship you're on now?" the old woman asked innocently.

"No aim for life-I'm coming for Death, crone- and every splintered off soul you have ever wronged for sport will help me get to you- If I have to trick you into sinking a barge to bring me there faster, so be it."

The old woman paused, caught in her fear game. "Who do you Think you are?" she asked, indignant.

"The one coming for your throne-" Artyo snapped.

The old lady purred, "You can't fight Fate... Child... not without an army the likes of which your simple, albeit rather more developed than most mind cannot not even bear to comprehend- a Plan-" the crone chuckled. "And any plan you create... is first drafted by the Anannke itself- you must accept it. Your gift of intelligence has blinded you to the holder of the pen dipped in the ink of your own blood-you will bow to me, bare your all to me, give me your throat, long before you can even-"

The old woman continued on, preening with the spiritual arrogance of a being who held every card she had ever known to be in existence.

"You cannot stand against the Anannke- the pieces of you necessary to even gain access to the Anannke are all but dead- and you need to see the pitfalls enveloped in why she would allow you to come anyway-" the blase crone murmured on.

"I won't have to stand for retribution- to repay It for what it has done, Crone...and your being here in the tattered rags of a itinerant preacher, still stained with the spiritual blood of those you stole them from...lets me know fate herself cannot stop- nor touch me." Artyo whispered, covertly closing her hand around a tiny coin that had spun towards her and releasing the one from the Anjuge with an absent flick of her wrist. "Enough of this!" She roared and snapped herself out of sleep.

Artyo rubbed at her eyes again, completely unimpressed by the theatrics of Fate trying to slow her down inside the synapses of her own head as she felt the rising sun dance across her face.

Her hand gripped the flipped coin without even looking at it.

chapter six

On the horizon the over-industrialized spirit of Buffalo looked dismal, as if it had come up short on too many steel age dreams to have kept faith beyond failing factories in the fallen angels who had promised eternities of riches via them. In the abandoned shipyards the beast that had carved the city from water and rock implored Artyo to make her way over to the bus station as quickly as possible in the half-light she disembarked in, praying that the blood and spirit spilled in its sister city would not continue on its banks.

The greyhound station looked consciously nasty due to new thinly veiled anti-tourism "travelogue" ordinances. Nevertheless, cross tripping in close quarters had become kitschy-chic for a certain segment of the population and no corners had been cut when it came to giving 4th generation urban professionals the roughing it experiences that fell in step with tales passed down from a time when people were still allowed to move as they pleased with homes on wheels chained to pickup trucks, even without enough for fuel in their pockets. Enough things that no one cared about had changed to make moving around like one couldn't afford to be tagged and tracked to fly cute. In most stations everything was covered with recycled gray dust that made sense with the stench of wet dog piped through vents for effect. Litter strategically gathered in corners stained with grease and sweat, and most drivers were hired through casting calls led by CSAs that had once booked character actors for over the top cop shows at the turn of the millennium. Artyo made her way back out to where the buses sat waiting for the hands that would start their engines that day.

She scanned the almost empty interior of the bus.

The smell of dog kennels and dirty people overrode all else as she climbed onto a bus that had NEW YuRK scrawled across a stained piece of brown cardboard stuck upside down in the front window.

About midway back on the left, a tiny old woman with dull eyes sat with piles of re-used waxed paper crumpled up in her lap, incisor-like hands covered with self-tanning stains picking sardines in oil from their tin and sandwiching them two at a time between melba toast before shoving them into the pitch-black hole of her toothless mouth. Feeling the photo-flash of Artyo's aviator-shielded high beams on her jaundiced forehead and tufts of wooly white hair, she looked up and smiled the sickly smile of an antisocial ancient who had offered one too many butterscotch candies to kids who disliked her due to their parents griping about her since they'd been born, an old lady who had spent twice as many years with that flavor on hand to piss them off as Artyo had been alive. A nod of understanding passed between the two as Artyo returned to the business at hand.

"Is this bus going thru Newark?" Artyo asked the driver, who was so lost in the brick wall in front of the bus coated with fake urine stains made with gallons of discontinued Marine eye drop solution and graffiti produced by kids studying the art history of hip-hop at prep school that she didn't bother asking for tickets anymore. No one was here in this hell she'd signed onto in search of a big break without meaning to be.

"-IS THAT WHAT THE SIGN SAYS?!," the driver snapped, not even bothering to look away from the wall that was the manifestation of the futility of her life in hell on earth.

A permanent scowl was tattooed across a face that had never gained enough weight to catch up with the catastrophe of the rest of the body that ballooned below. Artyo took another breath. She bent down next to the bus driver's ear.

"-IT SAYS NEW YuRK, not which hub it goes through- " she whispered.

The driver whipped her head around indignantly, clucking her tongue as she clocked Artyo's outfit disapprovingly.

"This is the 535AM-NUMBER 253- ALWAYS STOPPING IN NEWARK ON ITS WAY INTO PORT AUTHORITY!" the driver snapped.

The tiny old lady in the back snickered, sensing a battle royale coming, chunks of melba toast and tiny sardine bones sputtering from the side of her mouth and landing on her vintage Alice's Abstractions track suit as she did. She wiped them away bashfully, dull eyes suddenly shooting sparks over the possibility of witnessing a fight.

Artyo raised her brows above her aviators, looking at the crumbling facade that was her Steward back towards New York. The driver was bursting out of the uniform that they had told her to take care of twenty years ago when this job was new to her now literally " too big for her britches" ass.

She angrily fanned herself against the sudden onset of hot flashes with long fake nails with tiny charms glued onto them. Burgundy hair had been streaked, finger-waved, sister-curled, and French- twisted all over her tiny peanut head. Tracks of orange weave that she called blond kept getting caught between the folds of fat and fake gold that stained her neck with black marks.

Four pairs of gold-plated earrings hung in each ear, multiple rings leaving blackish stains on each finger. Her eyebrows had been shaved off and immaculately redrawn in maroon lip pencil to match her dye job, surrounded by hairs too short to be called anything but stubble.

"-Funny- that was Funny!" Artyo snort laughed like an old-school yakuza with no alcohol tolerance lit after half a beer. The spirit of death loomed out of Artyo's face like a naked skull.

The driver blinked in disbelief as the faces of every person she had ever known that had died flitted across the guffawing face of Artyo, the final flash being a reflection of the death that the driver started out each day hoping and praying for, on the road. Artyo shook her head violently at the now shared imagery of the woman twisted in an empty wreck on the side of the road, in shock and watching as her organs slid across the dirty floor from the gash in her side.

She slapped the driver's seat like it was choking to knock the vision out of her and then gave the bulbous woman a maniacal smile as she slid into the seat right behind her, choking on laughter every once in a while during their trip. She murmured approvingly as she watched the driver from the rear-view mirror throughout the entire trip the way ghetto kids stare at baboons showing their asses in the city zoo for behavioral cues.

The clicks in the yellow lines silently helped the driver find a reason for living again in the open road stretched between Buffalo and Newark, which the driver rolled into completely mindfucked.

Disappointed, the eyes of the old lady in the back eventually dulled back down, pulled out her old porn and settled in for her trip, a centerfold flipping open onto the pile of refuse in her lap.

Switching buses at the airport, Artyo rode the metro without incident through a Jersey City and Hoboken full of partially constructed skyscrapers and converted factories. The coast had been sold for glass beads and a bong to a New York City in need of expansion after so much of its territory had been left in ruins by terrorists, a sprawl fueled by decades of national pity, guilt, and relief that nowhere else was being targeted. The bombings did not spread to Jersey due to the ingrained belief that no one gave a fuck about it.

In Hoboken, she sliced through sanitized three-day weekend street bazaars along the docks, the sheer marketing genius of tapping into humanity's need for a little community, haggling and false sketchiness simultaneously, whitewashed to give suburban acolytes who had long since numbed out to the mall experience the rush of a raw deal. Artyo made her way down rickety gangways and cut a deal on a swiped wallet to ferry over sans ID chip to the Winter Garden, where she disembarked.

chapter seven

The door opened. The haggard Queen winced at the sliver of light that cut across the matted wall of silvery hair that formed her grieving curtains of state within her inner chamber.

The wardrobe of finery she had ripped apart in rage spread out around where she had remained in a heap on the floor for eternities, broken. As the Disappearance of the one who, to her was her child became official within the Pera complex murmurs of concern muffled themselves in the terrified throats of the courtesans.

"...Anything?" She cried out hoarsely.

"Not yet , My Mist-"the lead ANCs began in unison then froze as two caught sight of the gnarled twists of bloodless flesh that twisted up over the exposed, bare shoulder of the all but Queen of Heaven from violent self-flagellations within her Holy of Holies.

"Leave!" She roared viciously as she smote two of the three lead ANCs on the spot. The remaining lead ANC shook as it stepped back, head still bowed, covered in the ashes of its comrades as the rest of the guard behind him dropped to their knees and crawled backwards out into the main chamber.

"Find...my...child- I can't do this- without-" the broken Queen cried out softly to the only ANC who had given her the respect of averting its eyes.

"Yes, Mistress," The ANC who was called Tiburon

whispered before gently closing the door of the Holy cf Holies that was the inner chamber of the Queen.

chapter eight

The sky thickened as the sun rose over the western side of the city that was not what it used to be, but still was Manhattan. During the shortened work-week, Winter Garden was clean and packed with people too passive to blow their brains out in order to escape a rat race that had turned inside out.

On Mondays it was manic like the abandoned movie set of a futuristic utopian town square. Artyo crouched down on the compass cut into the marble. She tucked her legs under her and began to doze in the sun as past layovers rose up in her brain. Newspapers coasting on the wind replaced tumbleweed, degenerates replaced by slider thugs born of parents from places like San Fran and Seattle, after chunks of the west coast fell into the ocean, leaving only some of the badlands of Venice standing on the edge of the world. Early morn inner- city slider thugs-Mourners- swerved near her perch in the center of the concrete cove, like there was something in her vicinity that belonged to them.

Eating away at outer limits of their territory on old-school blades were Angry Adaptives, Yuppies of yore who'd invested too much time, pride and cash into the gentrification of the area before the attacks to be willing to give up so easily to the undertow of society skidding around on their marble piers. The more that the hyped-up wallets blading off weekend binges kept tempting fate for an ass-whipping by pushing into the pathways of the Mourners, the more the Mourners skidded towards her, cursing under their breath in both directions.

When in motion, the Mourners were invincible. they were oddly attracted to everything in the world due to how it seemed to call out to them as they whisked through it.

They were almost diplomatic, trying to not stain another stretch of pristine marble with the gore from yet another bloody Monday riot on the cove with hung-over, underemployed Adaptives looking for fights they knew they'd lose, so their bruised outsides could momentarily match their beat-up insides while they pressed charges. Again.

The skids on marble nearby pulled her attention out of her own crimes long enough for her to knock a slider or two off balance by the returned intensity of glares. Before anything else could develop, the Mourner ringleader rolled over and tossed a krill bar into her lap with an offertory grunt. The rest of his scraggly posse took heed with raised brows and gave her wide berth from then on, focusing their rising ire at being pent-in towards the appropriate Adaptive direction. Ripping into the protective foil of the bar with her teeth, Artyo pushed her aviators up so that they seemed suspended in front of her forehead, tangled up in the bangs they pinned away from her eyes. Artyo's eyes followed the ringleader as he slid away. He looked like Flea from Red Hot Chili Peppers before fatherhood hit. Harshly angled gray eyes, all the downy hair on his naked head, arms and legs bleached to the color of room temperature butter by the sun and Collodion silver now the norm in the drinking water. Silver bands stood out against the tan and tribal tattoos of his skin. Through the sheer muscle he wore she could see the blonde hair on his chest had black roots, giving the effect of hair floating above his over-defined pectorals. Beat-up baggy jeans hung from the bones of his hips with protective padding cloak-stitched into place in the folds at his knees, underscoring that "brains trumps brawn" thing apparent in many a tribal situation.

Faded residual memory-montages of lifetimes ago in Tokyo tried to play out without success due to the de- spooling program interrupted after being activated across Artyo's tongue. Nothing was left in the places they had once been found. Somehow, she made it to sleep anyway.

chapter nine

The guardian Kahn kept final watch over his charge, towering above her like a colossus. Wild in the wind, whited out eyes lined with kohl that reflected the bright orange of the sun climbing through the sky as she slept below him on the marble. His skin was coated in red ochre to cloak his signal, slick with scented oil instead of sweat. Kahn was unable to look at her without seeing where the splatters of the carnage that just came through her had stained her spirit. Pain was always infrared on her in his eyes, this time all the more. The only thing left to do was to wrap this up as quickly as possible. To silently help her destroy her own spiritual system like the rage-outfitted retrovirus she now thought she was.

She still tilted her head at the sound of him breathing outside of her. Like she did the first time she'd heard him utter a word aloud around her as a child. She still grinned as if she was the source itself in love at first sight with another soul similar to hers, as if it went miles in making the other things okay, blushing up at the still sweet sound of the separation of his thoughts from hers, in love with his love for her being such a given that it overwrote atrocity after atrocity in her life on Earth, in ways that went against every code tied to his initial spiritual position alongside her.

The beginning of this rumbled through his head as he bit down on his lip so hard that he would have bled if he'd been made that way.

chapter ten

The unconscious body of the princess plummeted down the abyss.

Her body caught on overhangs for a time that would then collapse under her weight, sending her further down in a shower of rocks that raced past and into her as she fell. When she finally landed, a jagged rock slammed into her face with such force that the scales upon her eyes shattered.

When she finally came to it was with a start. She inhaled roughly, blinded by white that crawled with black cracked veins on the inside of her lids and pain like she had never known above due to the bones and insides bruised by her fall. Suddenly she began to choke on a globule that rose up in her throat and threatened to force itself out of her ears, eyes or any other orifice if she did not open her mouth.

She realized that the black lines were her hair pressing against her face and wiped it away then turned and spat, opening her eyes for the first time. She was beside a trickle of a river deep in a cave that glowed with a strange iridescence. She choked up more, retching as the masses of quicksilver within her fought their way out, unable to stay inside of her within this changed atmosphere. Through cracked lens she saw the quicksilver race through the dirt in the dark towards the brook, fleeing the scene.

Woozy, she pressed her broken face back into the dirt and passed back out.

They surrounded her as she slept.

chapter eleven

Tiburon sharply turned and strode through the three units now wordlessly under his charge, his face on fire with clarified purpose. Each row he passed stood up and marched behind him through the complex towards the throne room. The cosseted nobility of the Pera complex scurried in the opposite direction as the ANC guard pressed towards the throne room.

A lone, bruised martyr balanced on a pedestal thick with rivulets of his dried blood in the center of the room, literally singing his heart out while tears of blood streamed down his filthy face. Tiburon looked over at the dais that had been empty for what felt like forever and scowled, indignant at the performance continuing sans the Mother of All,the One all the retributive work was for. The wastefulness of it disgusted him, the bland selfishness of the nobles made him indignant. With a flick of his wrist a third of the guard shut down the throne room, trapping all within it from the other side.

"Enough!!!" He roared, then snarled at what the sound felt like escaping his chest and echoing in the vast space around him and across the surface of the nobility. He motioned to his nearest guards, who wordlessly tackled the martyr from his pedestal by the throat and proceeded to stomp the swan song out of him so viciously that the courtesans tried to flee. The ANCs firebombed them to ash from behind as a cluster stood around the lifeless body of the one with the glyph Cleft tattooed on his arm to show who he was being martyred in honor of. Two picked up his body and threw it over the precipice as they all spread along its ornate edge to watch its descent, gleefully. Suddenly Tiburon flinched as the one place they had not scoured bellowed beneath them in his violently blank mind. He slammed down his helmet and leapt into the abyss, a third of his unit blindly following his lead.

chapter twelve

Third could have intervened long before she finally did, when it would have mattered. But she did not.

Kahn had built the Council of Thrones Complex with his mind and his bare hands. Hewn from granite, it was a huge amphitheater rammed up against a gigantic plate-glass wall that overlooked the red sky and ziggurat-styled super-structures of the Empyrean. In his mind's eye, First and Second were still leering at him. Hoods shielded their faces while Cossacks-free beings ashamed of not finding their appropriate place within Empyrean society that had become Punishers by default- were positioned around him, supposedly for Kahn's protection.

He had been "sequestered" as soon as he had returned from his extended sabbatical below and finished Puryf, then put on trial in front of the Council of Angelic Hosts in hopes that the pressure of his spiritual peers weighing on him from behind would get him to admit aloud what First, Second, and Third Head had not gotten out of him behind closed doors. He'd gone on a fast in defiance, refusing even water. The circle of peer pressure had grown until almost all the realm was involved without having a clue of what was afoot. The incense burning in the floor grates made him heady as he sunk into the memory. The flame-red sky seemed to stab him in his eyes, quietly accusing him of spiritual impropriety just as harshly as the Tryage.

The peanut gallery was full of residents of the Empyrean realm, including those on the edge like he had been before finally receiving his sabbatical, those who secretly spent eons in the D/o Theater Kahn had constructed as his Master Builder assignment in the fiery abode.

An assignment given as a gift by the same judges he'd ended up standing accused by. Angels had hung from the rafters to get a peek at the first transgression openly tried by the Council, the trial that quietly proved that many were as shackled as they felt in the realm the Tryage marketed as highest reaches of Heaven itself. Kahn had been web-shackled and shorn. He could still see his chin jutted out beneath his mouth defiantly as the memories rose up into his present reality. Still feel the death that radiated out of his eyes then.

"Records show that this was a CHOICE made by you and the one also implicated in this-" First Head Council had begun.

"Why would there be any records showing anything if there are no laws here to be broken?" Kahn had snapped, cutting First Head Council off.

Murmurs had shot through the cloud of witnesses as First Head bristled.

"Your exchange with - someone who had no rightful place in Heaven-" First Head attempted to continue evenly. The crowd gasped at even hearing the Empyrean referred to as Heaven officially, stirred by latent memories of the word from existences they'd been instructed to forget.

"You call this heaven- and it didn't happen 'here'- She protected Me THERE!" Kahn barked as his arm shot out in the direction of the Pera complex at the far end of the structures that spun out on the other side of the wall of glass. "You have NO authority there! And you have no Right to bind me here in this so-called Heaven!" He spat.

"Silence!!" the Second Head of Council had roared at the crowd. He then tried to continue where First Head left off. "You both have shown no loyalty to the hierarchy to which you belong. You seem- so enraptured by this objective to choose-so that which you exist by, you shall also be punished by-" Second Head had snarled as he had raised his gavel to pronounce judgment.

"Wait," Third Head had broken in, pausing the sentencing before all had been lost. "You are treating the- the theorized residuals of the supposed interloper Kahn may have brought here as if it is some sort of a plague! And the one that supposedly exists within the Pera complex has not even arrived here-She is no more of a threat to us than those subjected below. Kahn is not Elohim! His conjoining aspect no longer exists! It has been removed from Earth and will not exist in the Empyrean Outside of our assigning! -In honor of what has not been ordained by the Anannke sector where all this supposedly took place- we must be inclined to show mercy!"

"They touched! He touched her!" First Head bellowed.

"You have no proof there even IS a "her-" she interjected. "Her imprint is on his chest," Second snapped. "There are residuals of something all over his mouth!"

"What is on his chest and face matches Nothing that our records show has Ever entered the Highest High- so this purported She simply doesn't exist in my line of reasoning." Third stated calmly. "Look-He's deluded. After his Shabbat, He lost his mind in the re-Puryf process. The Anannke shows no knowledge of the She that he described under duress. He should not even be on trial."

Third Head turned to look at Kahn in the hushed silence of the courtroom. It had been the first time Third Head had looked at Kahn throughout all of this, knowing that the child assigned to him had called out to what Third actually was when she was on the verge of being lost and had been ignored, which is what triggered the intervention of this address, Kahn answering in Third's wake. Kahn and Third both knew that his interference was what he was really on trial for, not a supposed violation of the untouchable aspect of beings within the Empyrean realm.

Kahn glared balefully back into the hood that shielded the truth of what Third was from all those within the Council of the Thrones complex at that moment.

"Your options," Third Head had continued diplomatically, "are as follows: You WILL be made an example of, albeit temporarily. Repent, and once again become a servant to the council and your brethren-"

"Ah, yes..." Second Head agreed, audibly enjoying the arising entrapment as he entwined his bony fingers into a web of deceit that matched what he really was." -Or choice number two: Be consecrated a Zydduck- a wandering cipher, forsaking your slot within the Empyrean and your legionnaires, quarantined to Alt-land- the badlands between above and below, exiled, with no hope of pardon- your choice-"

Third Head looked away from Kahn. "As for this supposedly gifted child-"Third began absently.

"You want this suppressed!" Kahn exploded. "This isn't about her, or she, or Me- or untouchable status here at all!"

"It's about who you ALLOW to touch whom below and why! This council- you want slaves- slaves who breed more slaves for you! You're- You're useless without broken ones begging for salvation-You're SCABS blocking them from-"

"-Silence!," First Head had screeched at the ensuing uproar of the Angelic Hosts spread out beyond Kahn.

"You blaspheme US- our intent, our motives- In the name of- of this sniveling, defective child that no one wants-" the First Head of Council stammered.

"No! I blaspheme the ONE who gave you the power to ordain and institutionalize what those serving YOU did to this supposedly gifted child'!- God! I-" Kahn had hissed.

"GOD?" First Head had seethed, cutting him off. "GOD gave us no power at all- YOUR kind did, again and again-" he hissed back.

"That is enough!" Second Head had roared, cutting off First Head of Council before too much was said. "You have fallen! By CHOICE-choice!! For all in He- in the Empyrean to see-"

"You think the purpose of this dominion won't sink in?" Kahn had bellowed. "You think they won't figure out WHO YOU REALLY ARE?"

Third Head had jumped in. "Now wait- nothing has been-"

"No!!" Kahn screamed, pointing at Third Head of Council. "IT WAS ONE OF YOUR OWN, Third! I SAW THE- One

WIRED TO SERVE GOD -YOU-YOU OFFERED her UP-TO-to-save your-"

Kahn spun around and yelled to his brethren. "This is ALL A LIE! You are not where you think you are- you are not even WHO you think you are! Humans-they can get to the source without-"Kahn had appealed to the jury of peers. "We do this- We CREATE-create!! Every Single One Of Us! Just like them below-Sons! And Daughters! Children of- just as much as-I- she showed me it- a child showed me-we're the same- they're sons and daughters too- spirits like us- in different housings-"

"SHUT UP!!!!" Second Head had screamed ferociously.

"They don't ordain it!" Kahn had yelled to the Angelic Host, pointing roughly at the Council." They can't do any of it unless we give up and give them the reins! They only pervert things!" He screamed, flailing his arm back towards the triad of energies that ruled the Empyrean with an iron fist. "They are why the world below is so perverted! They are not the source of Inspiration or Assignment-"

"I will end this INSANITY once AND for-All" First Head had growled as he gathered himself up for attack.

"It can all be done without -without the- the guilt, the loathing-The Exchange- this Tryage -this sick Tent, so-called Tabernacle-attaches to it! And so can the ones we are Forced to look after but not Help when these sick Powers of This Principality set their sights on them-"

"Enough!!!" First Head had bellowed, raising his arms

overhead, a ball of spiritual fire growing in his hands as he lunged to smote Kahn.

"What are you doing?!" Second Head screamed, shoving aside First Head as he attempted to smote Kahn in front of the entire Assembled Host of Angels in the Empyrean, causing the ball of fire to swerve and hit the stand Kahn was spiritually shackled to. Upon impact, the web uncloaked and quicksilver chains on his nervous system glowed silver for all his kindred to see.

First had been pinned to the granite pulpit the Tryage ruled them from by Second and Third Head of Council as the heavy table of judgment fell from in front of them and shattered upon impact against the floor, impaling two-thirds of the Cossacks regiment surrounding Kahn from behind, reducing most of the Cossacks into piles of ash in front of everyone. Kahn's words and the proof of life they'd been given by the actions of First had the attending Angels still, in shock. They stared down into numbed-out limbs as their nervous systems momentarily snapped back on-line and began pushing the retrograde quicksilver that was in the water of the realm that made them want for nothing out through their skins.

"K-Kahn-" Third Head stammered, obviously shaken, still trying to pin down a writhing First Head of Council. "Kahn- Go!!"

The web of deceit restraining Kahn had dissolved and dripped off of him like sweat. He had grinned at the hushed crowd in a pool of quicksilver that had reflected his face back to him. "When you awaken, you'll be gone, too-" he whispered to the Angels, his eyes alive for the first time since he had died infinities ago.

"Vayo-Kahn- Go!! Please! GO-" Third Head had continued to yell at him.

"Do you actually think you will win?!" Second Head screamed, still trying to restrain First Head.

"Not only will I- will WE win- You're going to bring me back and beg me to make them stop. But by then, it will be too late." Kahn snarled.

"We have Legions against YOU!" First Head spat out from under Third.

"They don't even know that they're-" Second Head shouted. Kahn had looked up at First Head, his eyes shooting sparks of comprehension.

"-Neither do you-" he had whispered. His gaze had panned over towards the plate glass wall as a tiny truth registered inside him. "She knew..." He had whispered to himself in shock, "She's not-"

He paused inside himself before remembering the image of her that had come to him in the fast that stopped him from even drinking water. Turning back to the Angelic Host he shouted "Don't drink the water, Brethren! It's-something is wrong with the water-"

As he stood over the adult version of the tiny child who had inadvertently set him free, Kahn saw the mad dash he had made towards the window in his mind's eye. He had never known how the rest had come to be until right now, as his mind raced over the things he hadn't known his spirit had seen due to the reflective pool of quicksilver he had stood in.

He saw himself reflected in the whited-out eyes of his brethren on the periphery as he had cannon-balled through the glass, shattering the wall and his spiritual bodhi into splinters and streaks of TV snow mid –air.

The shocked wail of Third Head was drowned out by the gasps of the assemblies of Angels, and the sprays of the electric snowy residual had sucked back into the courtroom and splattered on the foreheads of pockets of those in the galley like fire, glowing like embers for a split-second before absorbing into them.

He saw scales crack and splinter off the eyes of some of the Others who had eventually found him below. One by one, they all begin to fall into piles of silvery snow to the horror of those seated around them.

As the Others had faded to the disbelief of the ones who had been too hyped up on Empyrean juice to process what had gone down to get out, First Head had barked out to the battalions of Angels remaining.

"Anyone else? Good- ORDER-! Order!" The voice of First Head had rung out as a new Table of Judgment manifested before the three Heads of Council.

"On to new business-" Second Head had tittered nervously as the remaining Cossacks were ushered wordlessly out of the Council of Thrones Complex. The crowd had realigned itself as a surge of bodies from the back filled in the seats vacated by those who had disappeared up front, already forgetting what had happened right in front of them.

chapter thirteen

The guardian felt his whited-out eyes go red as the remnant of that first Cossack brigade felled by his words and other's actions sprung up around him. His exodus had left the blood of their brothers on their hands, and reduced their job description to little more than henchmen and thugs, reprogramming that went exoskeleton-deep, clamped down onto them like giant bear- traps.

After eons of being force-fed blood lust and corrupted responsibility by a maniacal First Head who wanted to be worshipped as the only God in what was construed as its absence, they were true Punishers, no longer by trade, but by geist, a "score to settle" deep. Weaponry out, their eyes were ablaze with revenge for the fallen brothers and sisters Empyrean mandate forced them, on the threat of exile, to act as if never existed.

Kahn's remaining hairs stood on end as he crouched down into a low fighting stance over the curled up body of a still sleep Artyo. The Punishers swarmed as he slammed right back into the spiritual muscle, sending every one of them flying from the force of his re-directing counter-impact. Streaks of red- ochre trailed through the air, trying to keep up with his spirit, confusing the Punishers who actually made contact with the substance into slowing down as it soaked into them against their will and telepathically sent their every move back to him before they made it.

Weaving in between the arms and legs of the Firewall the Punishers attempted to erect, Angelic shoot-fighting skills spliced with straight-out street brawling had Kahn overwhelming the crew, as unaware of the Others peppering the periphery mimicking Kahn's every move in reverse and picking off the ones who kept falling back as the Punishers hit by them.

Kahn had violently knocked down almost half of those sent to bring him in when the air began to vibrate.

"All that will not be necessary, Zydduck-" a gravelly androgynous voice whispered out of thin air. The Others re-cloaked immediately, leaving Kahn to fend for himself.

The exoskeletons on the Punishers who were not already knocked to their knees rammed into them and they dropped down and covered their heads in reverence.

Vayo Kahn Diaz the rogue refused to bow, clenched his fists standing brazenly in the center of the Punishers and looked up into the sky around him defiantly.

"YOU know I did nothing wrong-" Kahn growled.

"You answered, Kahn-You were not in the position to answer her cries-" the voice continued.

"I am her Guardian!" he bellowed up into the sky. "Face me! Show yourself after casting the one wired the same as you down!!" Kahn bellowed up into the sky.

"To watch- You were sent specifically-To watch-" the androgynous voice continued.

Kahn screamed like a wounded animal as white flames smote him and those sent to bring him in out of sight.

chapter fourteen

The sky was the color of a blood orange split in two when Artyo was yanked out of her sleep by the dissolution of her guardian directly above her, violently awakened by the arc of her body through the air to the sound of screams and other bodies slamming to the ground. Flea-boy and a black slider boy called Obakegao [aka Ghostface] had grabbed her arms and tossed her out of harm's way before darting back into the fray.

A mealy-faced Adaptive lay on the spot she had been curled up on, screaming hoarsely. His mouth was a bloody gash of teeth chipped by the slider board Ghostface had swung into him for letting his hung-over friends cajole him into going up and seeing "...how tired the passed-out cunt really was."

Flea-boy and the Mourners had quietly swerved in his path to make him think twice to no avail, energy around them in a state of chaos due to the angelic ambush of Kahn that had gone on a few notches above their vibrations.

The Ignorant Adaptive had been like a piss-drunk frat boy, imagining how this antic would carve his cajones in the sky for sure, blind to the stifled screams of his friends as their bones were being shattered while he had eased into action. By the time the mealy-faced man had stood over her, the sun warming his upturned face while he undid his zipper, his buddies were already getting beat down by the Mourners who took the attempt on the innocent girl as the final straw holding them back from kicking everybody's asses.

Artyo watched in shock as the Mourners stomped the exposed penis of the Ignorant Adaptive to a bloody pulp, putting two and two together as she yawned through sputters of surprised laughter. The one they called Ghostface kept stomping the guy until Flea boy and the others pulled him off of him, the Du-rag over Ghostface's newly extended locks as sticky with the Adaptive's splattered flying blood as the Adaptive's own head was.

More Adaptives poured into the fray out of nowhere, screaming for the police and blindly swinging into the Mourner mix, burning off pent-up energies of their own in a battle on their home front. In a matter of minutes, the Mourners stood in a ring of felled Adaptives, scattered across another sector of smooth marble they knew they'd not be allowed on after all this. Blank-faced and raw, they all began to slowly slide off. Flea-boy circled Artyo's wrist with his boxy hands as he whipped past, popping her onto the back of his board as if an afterthought. Artyo's arms snaked around his midsection and she bent her knees instinctively as they all glided uptown like a swarm of bees drunk off a days' worth of nectar.

Ghostface slid up alongside them, motioning to Flea for his flask. Flea whispered to Artyo to grab it, and she slid her right hand into the upper reaches of his pants, pulled out the metal flask and tossed it to Ghostface, who slowed down to splash the alcohol across his split lip before screaming like a bitch as it resealed, speeding up so slicing through the air could cut the burn.

"Where thafuck yah Guard go, Tenshi?" Obakegao barked over his shoulder, tossing the flask back to her.

"Ghost ahead of me, I guess-" she yelled into the wind as they whipped through the remains of warehouses in the meat-packing district, taking a swig of the spirits so as not to be thrown off by wondering how he knew her name- that name in particular. He looked back at her over his shoulders, his black face glowing due to the white light spilling out of the spots where his eyes were supposed to be.

Artyo looked away, eyes shyly focusing on iced-down sides of genetically altered beef on display in the storefronts along the strip that had once held some of the trendiest gear one could find in New York, completely disinfected food the new true avant-garde.

"Wifyah wandering ron falling sleep outside wif Futant cut inya fo-head? I guessjah feels right on time dien, huh?" Ghostface growled, a chuckle weaving into his roar before it disintegrated into the blur of wind that exploded as they coasted into an underpass turned tunnel due to collapsed towers that no one had opted to rebuild.

Flea gripped her left hand tighter in acknowledgement of his first sprung status. His boys looked on as if nothing was askew, as if they'd been protected by Obakegao, the one they called Ghostface, for too long to not know offspring sync-up when they saw it. Artyo took another swig to cut the edge of seeing the offspring interact so out in the open, under the sun instead of underground. A mix of bile and alcohol burnt her tongue in the glare of the end of an Indian summer afternoon.

chapter fifteen

The cousins were discovered first.

The macabre beauty of the kind of child's place no longer safe or sacred for this current generation, a merry go round gleaming with all the bells and whistles worthy of your most favorite memories, sticky with blood. Surrounded by the cars of the ones who were killed prior a mass suicide. Sprays of blood across still gleaming headlights fifty feet away from most of the gore, with blood even on the top leaves of trees as if bodies had been dragged across them or blood had rained down from above. Burgundy imprints of palms on the trunks of trees,...and the ecstatic joy on the broken faces of the 38 girls and seven boys in the pile-up as if they had seen things with their last breath that made it all worth it.

Nameless kids dead by their own hands. It was a busy news day, and these were just another bunch of fucked up kids who had ended up dead according to the cops who had first investigated the scene, who had rerouted kids that looked kind of like this and that one in the pile to the impotent sex crimes precinct downtown over the years.

"Nothing new in that these days, nothing newsworthy," The policemen had assured the journalists as they spread the word to all divisions to buckle down-just in case.

They had left those bodies out there for hours after they'd been discovered out of indifference. Because the rumor that a strong easterly wind was coming that would make the scene not smell so bad, not stick to them like the guilt they felt about collectively not doing their jobs. Journalists stood around, bored, who saw nothing in the gore they'd long been desensitized to as worth chasing, ready to write it all off

as the rave gone horribly wrong the cops hinted it probably was. They hung out talking about ugly kids who needed braces. A small fire tried to kindle at the possibility of there being more to this than stupid kids hyped up on drugs that were being done across age and income lines just to get through life these days. Society had just gone back to Lord of the Flies basics, and it was pointless to broadcast the obvious.

Then the dots began to float up. In hordes, that looked like clouds of crows circling high overhead the other site.

"...Another site?"

That small fire grew as Ulteriors began to whisper in ears about cushy jobs behind a desk, in front of a camera, on a sound-stage doing lead-ins to the schmucks who still were stuck out in this fucked up field for not wising up and smelling the sweet scent of opportunity.

Tents were pitched. Spikes dug deep into ground still sticky with blood as writers compromised crime sites that wouldn't be inspected wholeheartedly anyway. Not after the first cops had spread the word. Suddenly, reporters who normally didn't even walk on grass without it being prepped for background viability found themselves climbing gore- splattered trees, going after blinking video camcorders hung up in branches on bungee cords, traipsing through both battlefields, tripping on rigor mortised arms and legs as they took digitals of ID tags that confirmed what the police had left to rot in the wind. The subject matter of the story wasn't seen as sacred. It was the ability of the story to elevate them all if they played their cards right.

Ulterior angels hung around the edge of the circus camp, egging them on, whispering how they could be the broadcast class of 2023 if they all worked together.

"Fuck it. Fuck the kids. The kids aren't the point. The story and what this story could do for our careers is what we need to coddle like a child. This is the story that could change everything for us As long as we tell the fuck out of it." The reporters agreed. And then it was on. The sound- bites flew to the North the East, the West and the South.

"It is a latter day Grimm's fairytale- but Black, blacker than most could believe-"

"The stuff that bad dreams are made of-"
"Like lullabies of children about plagues and being baked in pies long after it made any sense to their ears- stories that made sure children stayed safe in bed due to a perpetually placed mind-fuck-"

Once the parents were discovered decimated as if an enemy camp, and the documenting spools of the carnage were found scattered in baby-cams strung through the tops of trees, the lyrical beauty of lead-in sentences began to capture the hearts of journalists who had only gotten into the news racket out of a love for words in the first place, sensational words that made their souls soar and their egos anxious for the status that can come from a perfectly turned phrase offered them windows out of war-torn landscapes that they had never wanted to be trapped in from the beginning.

chapter sixteen

On the surface, the Empyrean went on as if the Kahnic exodus had never happened. Untouchable Angel societies swirled down the sides of the star until the hint of them read as flecks of blue in green under expansive red.

A large crow made a kamikaze arc in the thin air surrounding the Pera purification complex and dove at break-neck speed into the thickness of the atmosphere coating the skyline of the glowing city, gliding on low-level air currents above its golden causeways. The streets were canyons. Red skies seeped between what had to be the inspiration for skyscrapers down on earth. Standing as if chunks of cliffs that had been removed, buildings intermittently opened into rock-hewn gardens of visual delight. Trickles of green danced across plateaus in the distance, anchored by an oasis of trees here and there surrounded by metal carved sheets of stone, and glass.

Beautiful avenues crowded with untouchable beings. A non-abrasive esthetic coated everything that manifested here. Manicured hands slashed through the air expressively, near meticulously arranged "without a care" hair. Fractals of infrared light reflected off the faces of those milling around making noise but not really speaking to each other. The perfection of human bodies encased in cutting-edge clothing.

They sat smiling and laughing with one another, not ever truly having to worry themselves with concepts of intimacy or touch. A perfect place full of perfect people who had passed on, informed that they'd achieved a higher ideal in the process, and who'd stake their now never-ending existence on the truth contained in such information simply by a look around at their surroundings.

After-Life was beautiful!

A revelry of material happiness waltzed around them. Over-styled outdoor bistros and cafes lined the base of fairways, always ready to offer up a bit of respite in the midst of the perfection these beings milled around in continually. Menus full of fanciful dishes drew in the apologetically apathetic ones who silently struggled to come to terms with having no hunger, no honest craving they could place their perfectly sculpted fingertips on, in a designer world where designer meals went cold in front of last-life gourmands, preening with no purpose because everything was so flawless. All was beautiful! It had to be ...because they had arrived. All things were the same in their differences, creating a lowest common denominator that was so high on Plasticine that it was obviously rigged to blow, but the brunt of the Citizens of the Empyrean were numbed out to it.

It was the Choral effect. The rhythm the Empyrean reverberated to make everything observed seem symbiotic and singing in tune with everything else like the magic cure for a solar system's stutter. Classical music cat-scratched with techno pulsed out over the heads of Empyrean citizens who'd long since forgotten the ecstasy of being called to dance. Speakers were hidden from sight, subliminal sub missives woven into what was their now heavenly reality.

They resided in the district officially named the Empyrean- the highest high- the fiery abode of the Gods, what they privately called Heaven.

Everyone moved perfectly, aware of being watched by the cameras that were sprinkled atop street poles, making all on camera feel famous, forever, for real- and grateful for the closest experience to having an audience they'd allow themselves, only to shame themselves to the stasis that replaced sleep on the grounds of it. They moved as if tricked into some graceful dance for continual archives, in a place that supposedly had no laws to break that would require any type of surveillance.

The flow of heavenly Muzak was interrupted by the sound of static erupting across perfected realities like asphalt against tender skin, which happened more and more often as of late. Pirated Cryptic audio seeped softly out - a clandestine conversation between the Three Head Councilors of the Empyrean. Unaware that they were being routinely broadcasted. Twisted in the debate over how to handle the predicament that arose from the sudden legal but non- traditional influx into the Empyrean- children supposedly linked to original Other, Kahn, by varying degrees of separation.

"Full amnesia upon entering the Empyrean is the only road to take." offered First Head.

"A means of keeping the peace. We are in trying times. Heretics are acting out all over the place. Something needs to be done before it gets worse-" interjected Second Head as he nodded in agreement to the suggestion of First.

The voice patterns of First and Second were blandly similar. They were insidiously monotone- comparable to the tone of a shady politician and a scheming religious leader.

They were Wealthy men over rich coffee at the old boys club full of those who bought and sold bodies and spirits like others sold rice, surrounded by peers they would never have to explain their profit motives to.

"Once again, we all know no actual offense has been committed by any party, now don't we?" The one the called Third Head inserted herself into the conversation. Her voice was jarringly frank. Harsh, with a cut the bullshit clip to it.

"Why are you afraid of this one in particular? He has already run from you- why would you believe anything connected to him would ever consciously return?" Third said tersely. "What makes you think anything could be connected to him anyway- that he could produce without access his appointed Eloh-?"

"He did not run in fear-" First growled. "He left after cursing our dominion, promising he would return as you two pinned me down-" First snarled.

"You? Afraid of an Other's futile curse?" Third laughed loudly. "You were so enthralled at the idea of accessing his abilities to build ahead schedule- I had to erase all of him just to ensure you wouldn't enslave him."

First sneered. "Thanks to you- his Eloh was in the first clutch of them to jump ship-which is why you were supposed to erase him before, but did not- I have even heard whispers of your involvement in his sudden absence below this time-" Second Head murmured accusingly towards Third.

"How would you know about any supposed absence if you didn't know where he was in the first place?" Third mocked the other members of the Tryage. "I mean, really .. .expecting him to come through traditional routes- sneaking into Pera like thieves, checking in on all Possibles during their re-calibration sequences- you seem to want silenced a sound you've spent eons pretending that you've never heard." She murmured. "You're employing disarmament tactics against ghosts."

"Look-Back to the issue at hand-These children killed themselves to gain access!" First Head snapped.

"No-they found themselves the victims of violent acts that they had no choice but to remove themselves from-" Third Head countered.

"After the explosion of acts they blatantly instigated -" Second head stated flatly.

"As if they were synchronized-" interrupted First Head.

"-And where would a specification against said variant of supposed acts be? " interjected Third Head calmly. "How is that possible thousands of miles away from one another? Are you starting to believe in telepathy too?" She snickered.

"Third, you are just letting the tactile romanticist in your makeup run rampant, aren't you?" snarled First Head. It was the equivalent of the label counter-revolutionary being lobbed in Mao China. By Chairman Mao himself.

"This has nothing to do with the level of my sensory capabilities-" Third snapped.

"No, it has to do with that female ideology that is irreparably woven into your crosshatched mainframe- It was only a matter of time before your subjective issues openly overrode your-" First muttered under his breath.

"Not a surprising attack coming from one bent on finding a way to inspire from above all things that will lead to the justification of gender- genocide below!" Third roared.

Second stepped away, taken back by her sudden ferociousness. "What are you daring to accuse me of?" First barked.

"Of being the source of all of the banalities present in the age you covertly preach to have dominion over- as you make moves to manifest such a reality!" Third yelled, blackened teeth bared.

"Both of you! stop it!- What is all this?!" Second interceded, louder than the both of them. He continued in the saccharine tones of a seasoned bureaucrat, "Regardless of any opinions any of us have on the calamity that can erupt if this breech is not handled carefully, this remains the province of the Anannke for now!" First Head bristled against the pacifying words spilling out of Second's mouth. "When and if the situation trickles down to become a true provincial issue for us, it is under the providence of Third Head, not ours!" Second hissed, motioning towards Third. "Whether we approve of your decision or not, we must follow it until aggregate lots are cast per the actual situation."

You could hear Third's lips curl back in triumph across the

broadcast. "For now-there is no feasible reason for separating any of them. Let alone blatantly lobotomizing them, and you know it!" Third spat out. First Head glared at her again, silenced by Second's hand raised in objection of the start of a next round. "They will be kept together until we see how they acclimatize to our environment. We will go from there." Third growled.

The sound of her walking away faded out over the static of the airwaves. "You know..." Second whispered as Third disappeared down the corridor, in hopes of showing to First where his true loyalties lay in case the last exchange had brought him into question.

"Outside of the Original Other that our Cossacks lost the signal of so stupidly-it may be best to at least go and try to track the one that has yet to show up on radars above or below."

First raised a finger to Second's mouth in order to quiet him. "Ah! See, this is why you are here, to remind me of the greater vistas that must be considered. The guardian angels who went back on their promise by getting involved, who Had to have patched the little Suicidals in the realm in will be dealt with later."

"Exactly," Second purred. "And there are other interests that we must take into consideration...such as a potential Eloh for our pet Hezu-" Listeners could hear the slick grin as it spread across First's face.

"Amplify her Achilles."

The pirate broadcast booming across the upper reaches of

the fiery abode ended. The 'recently reconfigured to be beautiful people' fiddled around in the sudden silence between the end of the simulcast and the return of the heavenly Muzak. Their voices rose in forced revelry as they collectively attempted to block out things just heard.

The Council's cloaked modus operandi to thwart human advancement at any cost other than the one that required the Council as definers and mediators to said advancement, and guardians assigned to ensure each stayed the course was the undercurrent to the smooth Muzak that sailed across the skies of the Empyrean. The so called guardian angels that lounged around the Empyrean as Citizens waited for assignment as the hand's-on thwarter of an individual human's allotted progress, subliminally programmed to pay back any child of man still trapped in Hell on Earth for whatever was secretly held in Angelic hearts from before they had crossed onto better things.

The ones who somehow rejected the full reprogramming upon entry into the realm, not even of their own accord, were sneered at as Denizens. Some of them were already missing. Flyers hung by the Elohs and 'Hims left behind subversively littered Denizen-oriented areas, milk cartons bought above out of earthly habit were plastered with black and white photos of those who hadn't been seen in the wake of word spreading about the one once called Khrys.

Like earthly urban myths, stories of Suicidal Angels jumping flashed between those who would 'never do such depraved things.'

"Supposedly in droves... turning to liquid mercury upon breaking back through into the Earthly atmosphere. A rain of quicksilver-"

"Angels casting themselves out of this~ this- Heaven? Pullleaze-to go back to what?" droned a Citizen in repose over finger foods with Nan a fingerprint on them as he brushed even the idea of it aside. As above, so below.

chapter seventeen

Ghostface's tribe dropped Artyo uptown. Flea gave her the most innocent goodbye kiss of her life, the way offspring got when close to others different like them, foreheads pressed in camaraderie, flickerish in ways that kept fluid exchanges to a minimum. She spent most of the night in the burnt-out memorial pews of St. John the Divine, blanked out on how she got there due to the taste of his lips, terrified, grateful she had been locked in. Due to where her nails had dug into the antique wood of the pews They'd find out who the interloper was in a day or two. DNA was a bitch. But she did not care. Not anymore.

St. John the Divine was the one place the Sector-sim now in search of her wouldn't overwhelm her in the absence of Kahn. Almost every memory of her life hinged on having felt him nearby, long before she figured out how to see him.

In the empty cathedral, stained glass saints of light spat homilies at her in the dark, reminding her of the war about to begin every time her mind slowed down and gave them the chance. They had welcomed her as usual to the hallowed blue light, taking her return to the spaceship as a possibility that she was getting closer to believing she was worth being fought over. Battlers of supposed good and evil spent the early part of the night begging her to pick a team to play on so that the correct punishment for her "crimes" could be meted out, but it registered quickly that whatever had brought Artyo there that night had nothing to do with being drafted as a mercenary by above or below. She sat in the burnt-out corner of a carved church pew, begging the spirits hovering to shut up. Blue light made her jaggedness seem ethereal to the onlookers she felt there but could not see, braced against punishment that had nothing to do with the massacre she had just set off. Her mind wandered towards thoughts of Thyaz.

Thyaz had been the only full-on Other she had crossed paths with down here on Earth. Spawned from who knows what, but there all the same, for all with eyes to see. And he had spent five years attempting to mindfuck her for being able to out him so easily. He had run wherever he could to not feel the weight of her stare, had never wanted confirmation of what he was. Preferred a life in lieu of taking responsibility for steering the power that he preternaturally had. After clocking 85,000 miles in bounty hunter-like pursuit of the Dominican bastard, rescuing him time and time again, she'd finally stopped giving chase.

And now Punishers beamed his cries onto her. He was her Achilles heel, torturing her with a front row seat to his demise half a world away.

She felt Thyaz's blood coursing with poisons in Japan as if it were in her own veins in NYC, having no effect on him outside an erratic pulse, thanks to the awakening of his Ka. His screams of frustration erupted out of her mouth and echoed around her as every pain intentionally inflicted on his body left no mark. He walked through every level of depravity possible on her legs, making her pace around the altar until they gave out under her, a flicker of release as she pressed her hot forehead to the cool marble along the base of it.

Like a heroin addict in the throes of withdrawal, his body

Alone in brothels in the bottom of Tokyo, he got for the first time that his survival through ascension sickness depended on chikai- On some tangible experience of closeness to one akin to whatever he was, just as her survival had when he had triggered the uprising in her. And he'd chased away the only one who ever felt truly like him, and with her, all the Latents and Awares that had bubbled up from the underground with her arrival on the shores of the floating world in pursuit of him no matter how much of a prick he was to her- Awares that might have been able to help him now.

When she couldn't close her eyes to the cowardly whines of affected Angels and soul-mates any longer, she climbed out of a gaping hole in the side of the cathedral wall and zigzagged her way back towards the bottom of Manhattan.

chapter eighteen

In the VIP section of an underground club in the meatpacking district, clips from "the legend of Billie Jean King" spun over the dance floor. Pat Benetar's "Love is a Battlefield" video played backwards on mute, on stacks of old Technicolor televisions. Black and white WANTED posters were strung up between propaganda shouting about how badly "uncle Sam wants you," all visually synched to a twisted Prophet remix of "We're the KIDS in America."

The Ulterior geist for the event chilled with the party promoters who hung out on the ancient vaudeville stage up front. Club-kids danced under strands of chili pepper Christmas-lights, hyper-x'd out of their minds in order to feel for four intense hours at a time. In the midst of wild party- goers the echo morphed at the hands of deejays avoiding the police above for dealing and doing on a day to day.

Artyo danced like a banshee in her aviators and the thong that was stripped down to as the costume de rigueur for that nights festivities. She was in the dingy little spot that had once been hallowed as Jackie 60, where 60 bullets had once ripped through a wild girl's body, only to leave her still standing, to the shock of the abusive ex trying to gun her down in the first place.

When the crowd got too cute, she headed to the boys bathroom and pushed through lined up men in boxers and tube socks. Guys in fruit of the looms gawked from urinals they were too fucked up to use in the first place as she doused herself with water. Artyo smiled lewdly at them as they drew back in shock at the greenish glow they'd swear later they had seen hovering beside her.

She pulled on trade-gear benignly switch-lifted from a chola who'd admired her look as they were both made to take it all off at the door. The skintight slurred leather blazer, tight pencil skirt slit up the side and tailored to draw more attention to the other chola's newly doctored-up ass, and dainty drag queen stilettos that held on for dear life with the assistance of black silk ribbons bowing at her Achilles heel fit perfectly.

In a blink she was sitting at another spot, a piano bar hidden in the basement of a nondescript Con-Ed skyscraper near Chambers Street. Many years ago she had become a hostess for a night to see what the Gaijins who weren't under contract did to live in the bowels of Tokyo. Since then, the subtlety of the environment calmed her nerves. The sexualized aspect of it was no big deal. She had been indifferent and Aware since early childhood anyway. And the emotional side of it? The undercurrent of expected physicality played out as almost innocent, courtship.

Most men who sought out hostesses had gone through so much traumatic shit growing up that they were unable to connect in normal ways anyway. To show that to a wife would have been proof that the horrible things done to them as children really had sucked away all but a shock of outward masculinity. Most men in her global generation were so disconnected on the inside in order to survive that they could not comprehend anyone showing love or gentle compassion for them without a very real, fiscal cost attached to it. Love that showed up freely was a painful reminder of how crippled they truly felt, one that they strangled, beat and bludgeoned until it drained away. They were lost boys no one allowed the space to heal, and as they matured, they found money could be soaked in the same violent energies and traded on with half as much force, and that the surest way to save someone who dared to show love to them in spite of how the men treated them was to go to the whores that were paid by them to give it, so there was no confusion on either part.

The bartender reminded Artyo of loner ex-lovers in Shinjuku. He was too big to be anything other than a Offspring of Tengu-an illegitimate child of a Ronin daemon with no wars to ferociously claim allegiance to. The rough lines of his face made the doe-like beauty of his eyes and the gentle way he held his mouth still read as manly. He couldn't hide that he could hear the noise seeping out of her as she sat perched on a tiny cushioned chair at the end of the bar, even with the soft, uneven fringe of just been laid hair casting shadows over his lightly lined eyes as he looked at her on the sly.

It seemed like he towered over her, bony but broad shoulders hunched over English conversation books he kept behind the bar for slow nights. He looked like a sexual wraith twisted around in the pit of him, exposed arms colored with the slurs of brightly colored tattoos gotten too early in a yakuza life he had been lucky enough to escape the grip of in the impending collapse of New York. Something in her gnawed at pressure points behind his knees, making him want to bow to the insane reality whirling inside of her the way men who ended up in her bed had. She sat stock-still as visuals tilted around inside of her, fighting against a final delete. The bartender begged for an end to the cacophony inside her like a Shinto medicine man silently strung out in the wrong pocket of time, powered by the spirits of crows, crying out for some variation of Angel Dust to tranquilize them both.

Beautiful Japanese women worked their worldly intellects like charms over homesick businessmen stuck in NYC to save corporate face until the collapse of the world as they all knew it was final. Artyo's height and ordering plum sake and edamame in rough Nihon dialects kept them in check as they coasted on the sounds of flame-haired English Roses serenading the drunk number-crunchers with lifeless renditions of jazz classics.

Long bare legs crossed, ribbons at her ankles rustling under stares from salarimen with unchecked tendencies towards foot fetishism, the businessmen behaved with decorum as the sake-beer boilermakers hit them through intravenous drips while being fed bits of sushi with tapered fingers offered to discreetly suck. She tried not to doze as she watched oscillating shadows on walls from art deco fans spinning on tiny tables scattered throughout the place.

chapter nineteen

Anadyr lay tangled in sheets as things he was no longer allowed to call nightmares ripped at him. In his minds' eye he could see his consort IIrys in the viewing room of the almost empty D/o theatre, transfixed by the projection of the world below hologrammed in front of her.

The IIrys he cried out for was on the verge of succumbing to the call that rose up from the hole in the floor that allowed in broadcast waves from the realm some felt they had been forced to leave behind, respite from the fake perfection that one never spoke about.

Anadyr felt pressure in his chest mount as his eyes locked onto IIrys' hands gripping the armrests of her seat so tightly that her nail beds bled mercury. He called out to her as her hair danced towards the hologram in front of her. He tried to ignore what was pulling his assigned Eloh up against her outstretched arms, hands still bolted to the chair as if the last place the two had touched was the only thing that held her there, kept her from jumping away from the insanity of a false paradise.

A severe peace fell across her features.
"...follow me- " IIrys whispered over her shoulder. "No!!- IIrys !!wait-!!! "Anadyr screamed out towards the IIrys in his head.

Anadyr woke up in a cold sweat, the imagery of IIrys leaving him to rot alone in the Empyrean pounding against his head. He scrambled out of bed blurry-eyed and clumsy, still blinded by the imagery of her making her way towards the siren song of lives they had consciously left behind, away from what should have been bliss with one another.

He tripped over the straps of his re-adjusted cyclist shoes as he pulled micro pore pants on in a panic. The paintings that lined the hallway slammed against the floor as he stumbled towards the door, his head twisted up in the arms of his filmy hoodie. Terror-stricken, he exploded out into the empty infrared streets.

follow me, Anadyr- echoed against his eardrums, pushing him even harder than his old heart would have thought possible. He couldn't lose her- he refused to lose -The deeper he ran into the under alleys of the Empyrean, the faster the image of the IIrys in his head seemed to move away from him, as if she could feel him.

She looked over her shoulder as she hung in the air and smiled benevolently. " follow me-" played across the surface of her lips as if on a loop. She could not hear the harsh gasps for air exploding out of his chest- she couldn't hear him at all, only felt him finally coming after her, and it galvanized the heart- filled decision she had made to finally exit this god-forsaken place.

Clusters of dysfunctional entities who called themselves Denizens streamed past his peripheral vision the deeper he ran into the catacombs of the Empyrean, the district of initial untouchables. Beings that found respite within the ruins of the first ones to fall out of favor with the Empyrean enclave solemnly started their assigned bliss on the sight of him being devoured by his own unspeakable panic each time he ran by, so accustomed to seeing him cut through the air at what they referred to as "that moment" again and again, that they

clandestinely used him as a timekeeper in a place where watches were quietly outlawed.

They sat waiting for his passing in plazas that also never slept, coated with stoic spiritual faces Empyrean citizens would consider heresy on the upper causeways.

Acknowledgement of his silent grimace against the force of his own fear was the closest many came to rebellion outside of locational association. His terror run had become the pace of the only peace they'd found in so-called heaven.

"follow me, Anadyr- you –o- ere to find me- "IIrys whispered in his head as his mind's eye saw her balanced on tiptoe atop the old-fashioned banister that rimmed the balcony.

The connection began to break up as she was pulled up off of her feet by the magnetic field of the wormhole that gave them ocular access to the world below this one. As the connections between them dissolved, his pace quickened and his pulse slowed down. Atoms of his own soul broke off from him as the remnant of her leapt out of the system.

He silently cut into the courtyard that led to the Demiourgos Theatre Complex. His body slammed into the cuff of the pulse-pass code reader in the gate. Entry that should have been automatically programmed produced nothing but the memories of what the pain of running headlong into a brick wall by mistake would feel like. Anadyr slammed against the membrane separating the keys to the D/o theatre and the gatekeeper from sight, rousing the wizened gatekeeper from what always felt like the heaviest non-sleep of his manifold existence.

Ahsa, Anadyr-" whispered the old man who had chosen to manifest the unspeakable beauty of the latter life in a realm that thrived on the opaque aesthetic of all things young as he slid the newest personalalt-access stamp to his most concentrically traumatized patron. Anadyr bent over his knees and pressed the new code into the flesh of his forearm as his breath shuddered out of him. He then placed the sliver-thin dissoluble stamp on his tongue LSD-style and felt his system recover from the expenditure of energy that had gotten him through his run.

Eyes slammed shut, he found his way into the seat she always occupied in the dream that had tortured him out of stasis ever since she had escaped without his rising to follow her. He dragged his hands across the ridges left by her fingers, the only thing that let him know that she really had been holding on for him to get there. He made himself sit still as the projection system whirled into gear.

The sparse white light from the hole churned before throwing up the image of Shinto temples that had gotten his beloved so beside herself. Since they were assigned Elohim, the codes of ANAdyr & IIrys combined in the D/o theatre, so the residual montages that tore him apart were a splice of things they both had loved to see and miss below. The climax of the personalized horror movie was Anadyr seeing the bliss on her face as her body dropped through the floor- the last entry she had made into the program.

Then all of Anadyr's fear imagery kicked into hyper-realistic action. He saw Angels falling from heaven to earth, soaked with the blood of rebirth. He imagined the impact of his IIrys, in some craggily field in Northern Asia.

He saw her blood soaking into the ground, making it verdant as it devoured the remnants of her. He saw first the altars and then temples and finally great cities that had been built up over the destruction of her, the trickles of her life force into the waterbeds of the region that bloomed into sibling cities, her offspring without him, the things that grew out of her second demise.

And as usual, he vowed to never forgive her for leaving him. Let alone for leaving him to explain. He wallowed in the pity of her absence, and it numbed him to the realm he was expected to participate in regardless, as if she had been entwined with him now. It prepared him, filling him with enough animosity to plow through potential assignments of the next stretch.

When he walked out of the catacombs, bazaar, then back onto the upper causeways of the Empyrean, the newest crop of untouchables didn't make his skin crawl with their false celebration. His anger cut a path for him, her absence the only shield to get him from place to place amongst these beings that had been the kinds of people he had already found despicable down on planet Earth.

Entering the lobby of his building, the doorman inquired about his run without looking up. Anadyr walked past as if he had heard nothing at all. He pressed his palm into the door to his sanctuary, the idea of stumbling across pictures and plants appealing to him. The door easily swung open as everything that had been knocked out of place had been returned to its original position.

He swore under his breath, the words tumbling from his

lips as "Well gosh-darn it heck!" with the lilt of a shamefaced smile that had nothing to do with the scrawl of hatred across his perfect face. He kicked on the writing on the wall- messaging unit. In red above his bed was written:

"ANAdIIrys- as part of your service to the community of citizens within the Empyrean, you have been assigned as comptroller to an entity possibly entering into said Empyrean-"

A joyful "Well golly-gee!" came out in place of what Anadyr cursed. Exhausted, he stripped and crawled back into bed, throwing his arm wildly over the edge and rapping his knuckles against the steel toe of the boots IIrys had always told him not to leave so close to where he always fell out of bed.

"I'll be a monkey's-" He screamed in attempts to curse before he gave up. Anadyr spun around under the comforter to glare balefully at the offending boot from the edge of the mattress.

"You will be expected at the arrivals gardens at a soon-to be specified time. Prepare accordingly." was scrawled in black across the stretch of the concrete floor that he and IIrys had left around the bed. Anadyr sighed and stared up at the ceiling. The sheer membrane their respective recalibration programs were woven into hung from the rafters like a mosquito net eons after it has outworn its use. His fingers danced across the slippery surface closest to his face as his mind tracked down thoughts he'd never let himself complete when she was there.

His nails dug in more as he stared at the contraption that kept them from touching even in bed. It hung listlessly, mocking him the way it did when she was a yard a way as cleanly as it did in this infinity-cursed abyss she had now created between the two of them. A tiny voice in his head that he knew was hers implored him to break out of this heavenly hell and rip down the membrane that had kept them trapped together in it, but apart.

Angrily, he ripped at the scrim, scratching his own forearms with the ferocity of his outburst. A howl exploded out of his chest, his throat burning as if he had just inhaled ice-cold water.

Heaving, he dragged the back of his hand across his cheeks in loving memory of tears that had been blotted out upon entry to the Empyrean. The bizarre shade of vertigo that painfully reminded him of exactly how high up he was, and the things that were unofficially not allowed slammed into him, leaving him dumbfounded for the last time. His eyes narrowed.

Anadyr shoved his fist across into the forbidden territory that had been her spot in so-called heaven alongside him and pulled her bedding over to him. He shoved his head under the pillow that still smelled of the absent love of both his life and death and prayed for sleep in the memory of her wild hair harassing the sensitive skin across his cheek, lifetimes ago.

chapter twenty

Back at the Winter Garden, Artyo's heels clicked across bloodstains from that morning's battle that gleamed like oil on marble as she made her way to the yacht docks. She boarded a water taxi, inciting the captain to start his engines two hours ahead of his shift by sliding him the bills from the wallet lifted earlier that morn in Jersey.

She sat in silence, the mix of river and ocean lapping at the hull as tiny boats intersected in the dark. Artyo ignored the white clumps of sea foam that, with each blink, looked more like knotted clumps of hair with the drowned bodies of small children tangled within it, white hair glistening like corn-silk against the shimmering navy-black of the water. She was headed out to the Statue of Liberty, with a return ticket handed to her by the captain that took her to Staten Island instead.

The rest of the skyscraper canyons of Manhattan rose up across the waters, doing the best they could to present a united front. Smoke from chemical fires that burnt like eternal flames in city pits rose up like clouds being born off of temperate rainforests along the Pacific Northwest coast. The smell of inner-city was replaced by the light stench of sulfur. The view-finders that once systematically lined Battery Park now looked at Hoboken and Jersey of all places, sister-cities that had always stood in NYC's shadows. Large chunks of the man-made land at the bottom of the island fell away each day, old subway cars filled with debris drifting out into the Atlantic like bits of glacier during calving season, socio-techno icebergs made of urine stained newspapers, plastic bags, motherboards, and magazines. Attempts to rebuild a third set of towers on ground zero had finally stopped after an onslaught of serious seismic activity had made many atheistic islanders grasp for God.

The blue ghosts of the twin towers jutted up like a banner for Wall Street grifters that still made their money hinting at impending doom to richboys who had not noticed their own descent or that the end had already arrived. It was a realm of leeches sucking away mouthfuls of manhood with every dollar redirected, notches on headboards the cowboys refused to notice they were chained to, unable to spit or swallow.

The game had never recovered from its crash decades ago, instead becoming true to its pimped and hoed hustle between game boys, gigolos, gamblers, and grafters. The few trophy accounts left were hoarded like presidential stains on a dress. Coked up high-class hustlers still had trophy wives, trophy whores, and little blue pills that warded off the reality of not being able to get it up for either without lots of saline titillation and pharmaceutical assistance. Game boys got fisted by therapists as they droned on about how they only got hard when they came close to talking male clients into giving seventy percent of their assets over to the hot-shot company head the grafter worked like a whore for.

"-The kind of men Thyaz said he wanted to be like," Artyo mused absently. "Like he always said, the best way to fuck a man out of his money - is to call his masculinity into question against your own." she murmured aloud, finally affixing a name to the third-world born, hollow aggrandizing she'd grown weary of watching her flesh-filled soul mate try to clothe himself in.

The sky was a vibrant hue of ultramarine as they bobbed against the boards of the tiny dock at Liberty Island while she took off her shoes before stepping on the holy ground.

"But he's quickening-" erupted like car bombs in Megiddo in her head as his Ka chose that moment to rock Artyo's inner ear.

She forced herself to keep walking. "Like I give a fuck-" She hissed to his soul. "I'm done-I'm out of here. His ass is where? Fucking Sweden? Tokyo?-"

"Artyo- he's quicken-You know what that means!-" The Ka of Thyaz burst back in.

"Stop coming on this frequency-end transmission!-" she hissed to herself and turned to stare up at Liberty's shrapnel- scarred base in silence.

It was hot and the manicured grass was remarkably soft under her feet for so late in the summer. She made herself comfortable in the shadows, too far gone to question why she kept falling asleep.

chapter twenty one

Ornate strips of iron crisscrossed over a high ceiling set with uneven skylights. Hologram fire torches lined the walls between chambers hewn into the sides of cliffs. They reflected in the plate glass making up the wall opposite them. Gutters were beveled into the metal tiles where the floorboards would normally adjoin to the wall.

Tribunal had just ended. The two male members of Tryage nodded at the departure of Third down a hall and floated down the rotunda corridor as she walked away with her waiting attendants to take care of something brought to her attention by them at the end of session. The two men turned toward one another and began quietly conferring on the subject of the optimal candidate of bride for Hezuz-the Khrystos they were grooming for the end of times campaign, oblivious to a trickle of mercury that trailed them in the floor's gutter.

"You know Third will not approve of the pairing." Second Head started
"Not my concern." First Head countered.
"Head-" Second Head sighed. "...Why bother with -" "This was your idea initially!" pouted First Head.

"But not against her will! Overall I agree- her shall we say.. . prowess would do much to strengthen the outward ocul of Hezuz to the Citizens and Denizens, but did you look at the details of what she's done- she will have to be doubly broken down for one such as him to even be able to bear." Second Head lamented.

First Head sighed." What do you think was behind separating the two? I would never consider forcing Hezuz on her...but there is a lot to say about not giving her any other options- what a coup!"

Second Head scratched his chin. "Then it is done. I will prepare Hezuz for engagement- which is always imperative to do with such a charmingly slow specimen, isn't it? She will certainly not be what he has become used to temperament- wise." Second head whispered slyly. Both chuckled.
At the end of their stroll, the two looked up as the third member of the Tryage returned to the main hall to go towards her own chambers alone. The three rulers looked at one other impassively and went three separate ways. The trickle of mercury that tailed First and Second followed Third down the hall to her quarters.

Third Head walked in, took off her hooded cloak and slipped out of padded split toe shoes. She let out a sigh of relief at returning to her own territory. Bare feet sunk into tiger skins spread atop the heated copper tiles of the floor. With each ancient urban city blueprint stared at against blood red walls, some of the inane rhetoric Third had just spent forever smiling complacently through fell away.

White pleats of linen exhaled around her as Third unwound the indigo blue sashiko belt that held the fabric in place. Slubbed silk leggings glowed in the light from the fire pits within the floor. She put the space on lockdown in silence before sitting on a pile of pillows in lotus position, hems crumpling around her toes. The silvery trickle traveled across the floor and pooled behind Third.

"What did you ocul?" Third called out, eyes closed.

The one called Globyl rose up from the mercury puddle like a

futuristic water nymph, arms stretched above her head as if she was Venus rising from the foam of some heavenly sea. She was barefoot, in a denim micro-mini skirt that played up the blue veined tattoo of ley lines that spiraled up the back of her pale white legs. She folded her arms down and yawned as if the transformation had made her groggy. The aggressively slubbed sleeves of her silk knit sky blue top dangled near the floor and her platinum blond tufts of hair blew in a breeze that made up the laissez-faire aura around her. Globyl's eyes whited out from the buzz of information as her matte mouth slashed open and she began delivering her report.

"You were right." Globyl began, "The other Tryage members have insidious intentions of their own for the girl. They plan on ensuring that she is Elohim with the idiot Hezuz, no matter how she comes in."

A snarl fluttered across the face of Third Head. "Make things sloppier than they are used to working through to get what they think they want," Third snapped without opening an eye.

Globyl nodded, turned on her bare heels and ran towards the wall of windows that looked out onto the Empyrean cityscape. She slammed into and soaked through the walls, drenching the exterior of the building with the moisture of her dissolution. Outside in the Empyrean, it began to rain.

chapter twenty two

The Empyrean streets below were crowded with two distinct types of people.

Type A ran furiously for shelter as if acid was falling, disgusted. If Type A could have been able to recall how to curse, the sensation of the rain on their skin would have called it up.

Type B was frozen stock-still in the sudden deluge. Almost ecstatic at the play of wetness on bodies they'd thought were numb. Faces were upturned, mouths slightly slack, the bliss of sensation searing through them, the pure mercury that fell drawing out residuals of the retrograde quicksilver in their systems still present after so many had covertly stopped drinking the water of the realm.

chapter twenty three

A night guard came across Artyo sprawled on the grass at 330 AM. The plastic buttons of his gray uniform braced themselves across the expanse of beer-gut hanging over his belt. He was about five foot seven, a stone's throw away from being as wide as he was tall. His face skin was mottled in a way that made sense of the stench of bourbon that rose off it, the nose having spread long ago into the contours of a potato. His mouth sat open under a reddish beard still full of crumbs from the fifth meal of his six-hour shift the way the mouths of those who started out slow did when they let the years slide by without any correction.

He stared down at the contours of her body, entranced by the way it was encased in leather boning he'd only seen on techno-trader cards of Collodion-coated burlesque chicks. Her steel-spiked stilettos were loosely grasped by their ribbons, knees knocked together under the severity of the sleep that had toppled her. She looked like a discarded date rape victim, roofied beyond repair. The corset built into the blazer pushed up her breasts, shellacked animal flesh glinting against her coppery skin in the dark. The fabric of the skirt molded her lower body as if it had been poured over it. Her lips were lined in black and glossed over with M.A.C. Lipglass like a harlot. Reflective aviators hid eyes he was sure were almond-shaped.

He raised his left hand, the wedding band trapped on his finger between bulges of fat glinting in the moonlight. He hesitated as his mind's eye slowly caressed the beguiling fabric of her skirt, imagining himself sliding up its hem and taking a peek. Suddenly his nostrils were flooded with the scent of fried chicken, liver and onions, ice cream- everything he had ever gorged on in this lifetime.

He may as well have been in heat, sweating chocolate sprinkles. Heady, he was slowly bent over her as if he was worried she might disappear when something inside of him yanked his eyes up to the face the mirrored lenses hid half of.

"Touch me and you'll be dead too-" she whispered as she pulled her full height up over the frozen man. He smiled stupidly, embarrassed because he couldn't see her eyes and was unsure of how much she'd read in his face. For the first time in years the instincts of his bloated hand overrode the sloth that had enveloped him, absently reaching for the nightstick that his mind's eye had to remind him was protecting his flask at his desk instead of sitting in the loop where it should have been at his hip. As her smile flashed him, the faces of everyone he had ever known seemed to ricochet across the surface of her. He took a small gluttonous step back. Reflexes that had been dead under layers of flesh and alcohol for years throbbed under his now wet skin.

Bloated guardians sprawled around him in the spirit screamed at him between sloppy mouthfuls of fed-upon flesh that he was in mortal danger from what was forcing out that grin before destroying anything it danced across. Their atrophied legs spread out under folds of flesh that poured from distended bellies, the air suddenly rancid from the smell of rotting food caught in wrinkles. She cocked her head to the side, sensing nothing predatory about him, wondering what it was that had led him to even think of coming towards her with outstretched hand. As she did, she saw the slovenly spiritual corps feasting around him in the spirit that had encouraged him towards his current obese state.

She threw up a bit in her mouth as she saw one violently grab the hind legs of a little lamb that ran through the field of gluttony, roughly break its pelvis, rip the tiny animal in two and ram the still bleating raw meat of the babe into its abysmal mouth.

"Watch out for that one-"the obese guardian chortled as it dragged its blackened teeth across the now red wool tufts it sat choking down. Another portly guardian heaved itself like a walrus closer to the one asphyxiating on wooly hairballs and slammed a log-like arm against its solar plexus.

"Something is wrong-it's not the right-why are you blocking- something is-"the Ka of Thyaz boomed up again inside her ears.

"End transmission-" she hissed again and bent over, dry-heaving, confusing the night watchman and the terrified angels of gluttony spread around him.

"She's about to blow! She's about to blow-" the gluttonous guardians wheezed, exhausted from the exertion of pulling themselves the equivalent of two steps away from the fray. Horrified, they did their best to get away from him and her with one bloated hand like giant jabba-the hut-like slugs, shoveling handfuls of grits into their mouths with the other as tears streamed down from their eyes and gravy from the corners of their mouths.

Baffled, the explanation tumbled out of his mouth before she could even think to ask. "I wasn't going to touch it-I didn't think you were real-" he stammered. "Please- I have a family- a grandkid-my stupid sonafa- kids- I love my wife-I'll leave you alone-Please forgive me-" He wheezed, " I don't care why you're here- not for 7.50 an hour- I don't see you- I'm too old-

I just want to retire-You're not real-I just want to go-home-" The pudgy man cried out and started to sob.

"Come on! Let him be!" his obese guardians whinnied further away from any possible fray but back to sprawled positions on the grass with replenished buckets of hot wings and fat- backs, his tears both ruining their appetites and pulling the trigger on emotional eating at the same time.

"Yeah, leave him alone-,"
"He didn't have anything to do with it-"
"Only thing he's ever molested was a bucket of chicken and a pie-" a beast snorted.
"And he's so sorry about what he did to that pie!"
"Maybe not the chicken though- that chicken deserved it-"
"Just go! We won't tell!" croaked another around a handful of mashed potatoes.
"We'll cover-"
"Yeah, We didn't see nothing-" sloshed another around a mouthful of vanilla pudding.

Artyo looked up, repulsed by the sounds of chewing that surrounded the two of them. "Promise on his life." she demanded, calling out to the things he couldn't see that he was bound to.

"Aight! We Promise! We Promise!" the spiritual slugs cried out in unison.

Pushing her sunglasses up on her forehead, Artyo and the guard looked at each other, her eyes as tired as his.

"Stop listening to them. They only want you alive so they can get credit for feeding you to death." She whispered.

The guard nodded and waddled away as if she had never existed, stomach rumbling. The heavy guardians dragged themselves behind him.

"I think he brought ribs for breakfast. And PIE." They called out to each other as they slid into the mists of early morning.

chapter twenty four

Anadyr woke from a dream to the cacophony of one hundred bells outside of his door. Hot tears still careening down his chiseled cheeks in the dream, he slammed two more pillows over his head, pinning himself against the imagery of tears with his forearms.

The heavenly bells grew louder and louder until the neighboring Denizens above and below began to scream niceties up and down at him in place of the curses they were trying to lob.

"That sure sounds important!" "Golly gee!" "Go answer the call for the love of -"

Eyes narrowed, he crawled out of bed and made his way down the hall towards the noise on the other side of his door. As his hand sunk into the appropriate exit ID indent, the overwhelming racket ceased. The door swung open in silence, not a soul anywhere near the entryway. Anadyr gritted his teeth and tried to slam the door, which softly closed in spite of him.

"Thank You!!!" bellowed from above and below, a saccharine chorus as transparent as the envelope edged in gold that had blown across the threshold unbeknownst to him when he first opened the door. Bleary eyed, he crouched down like a Japanese kid whose parents hadn't told him it was impolite to squat outside of the bathroom no matter how comfortable it was. He rocked back on his heels and fell softly into the wall. His eyes went to the last painting IIrys had wanted to see whenever she left the space.

The red ochre blurred with sienna, squash and swirls of brilliant blue. The form of a woman was woven into the reality of the landscape that she seemed coated in, victorious in the absence of anything else around her. Anadyr remembered being only slightly impressed by it when she lugged it home, more moved to mirth by her continual flogging of the non-rules every other entity seemed so happily impinged by in light of all else wrong with them ending up there together.

He remembered her softly reaching for his chin, her eyes soft with the shock of him not even feeling her clandestine caress as she tilted his head to the side. It was only when you cocked your head to the side that you saw the swirls of blue denoted a series of hand-prints peppered across the woman's flesh that were so beautiful that it was visually obscene. A chaotic signature that began with the letter "S" was tangled into the pubic hair you only saw at a 70-degree tilt or less. The electricity of the old touch that he had blocked then crackled across his chin and cheek in his present moment. Anadyr's eyes grew steely as he picked up the official notification of the impending arrival of the being ANAdIIrys had been assigned as comptroller to.

Hyperbole on the effectiveness of audits and impending prosperity in a realm where one desired nothing at all came with the assignment to one of the saved millions blurred in front of his eyes as it rose up in him.

Anadyr blocked the accusation that it was supposed to be IIrys' turn to play "lying son of a- be our guest-" to some newbie who bought into this feels like heaven sack of-" He stood up and made his way to the kitchen.

He wondered if others had known and cheered her on while he remained in the psychotic numb state he had fallen into to survive being there at all. He beat himself up until he had dehydrated himself and then oddly prayed for the presence of, of all things, lemonade before opening the refrigerator, the first prayer of his life on the other side of death, where all need to pray was supposed to have ceased.

Lemons cascaded from the interior of the fridge and rolled across the tiled floor.

chapter twenty five

When the princess reawakened, she stood up in the dark on legs that only got firm when why she fell came back to her in a reverse flash, culminating with her hand slamming in to the pale prisoner's sternum.

She grunted against an awareness that coasted through her body unhinged, pure. Whatever he had done to end up in chains under the attack of the Queen mother had set her free in a way that was impossible prior to every moment of eternity that proceeded it, and she would find him, somehow, so he could explain how.

Chin pressed to clavicle, she shook her head a bit. The last flakes of the scales that had shattered on her eyes with her final impact dusted her decolletage, stinging as they hit her bare skin. It was the first moment she realized she was naked except her obscenely long hair, which draped itself protectively around her like a tangled yet glistening black robe. All of the jewels and gossamer she had been adorned with upon being put to bed post-blackout had been ripped from her body as it roughly slammed down the jagged walls of the abyss.

She absently brushed the scales off of her chest and centered herself by looking down at her palms the way she had always done as a child of the Empyrean. She startled as the faintest line rose up to the surface of her translucent flesh halfway between her left thumb and spindly index finger and seemed to pause as if waiting for acceptance, or direction. Whorls pressed forward in bas-relief at the now daintily padded tips of her fingers. Anger flooded through her as splinter memories of the atrocities she had seen the Queen of Heaven cheer on smashed into her in this strange atmosphere, as it if were permeated by the collective pain of every discarded instance of cruelty that had been enacted for pure entertainment. They soaked through her like the smell of sulfur, disoriented her to be in the midst of en masse.

She didn't realize she was being propelled by it in the dark until she was nearing a bend in the cave and found herself retching with her forearm and face pressed against the dampness of it. It was her disgust that had forced each step forward, away. She turned the corner and saw light, alien to the incandescent red of the Empyrean sky she was raised under. The faint hum of it registered to her eyes as greenish and she was both alarmed and steeled by it. She inhaled sharply as the memory of her wet nurse smote to dust right before her eyes racked her senses, followed by the dispassionately obedient, caged faces of the ANCs.

Nothing. Remember. Run.
She had to move. Now. And knew it.

chapter twenty six

Artyo watched the sun rise on the pock-marked feet of the Statue of Liberty. She looked up at Liberty one last time, knowing the path she was to cut would take her towards a freedom the greenish black goddess could probably never have comprehended. It was already apparent that it was going to be a blistering hot day for the middle of September. She headed down the rickety planks and boarded the boat that crossed the waters to the Staten Island Ferry station, changing for the ferry back over into Manhattan.

At Staten Island Station, the first half of the morning shift filed past like sheep. She watched, hearing nothing but the churning of motors. Eventually, the commuter ferry into Manhattan was crammed with its a.m. road-ragers chained to commuter cups.

Coffee bought from the gnarled old woman in the dirty storefront near the dock sloshed onto already stained cuffs and seats as the boat swayed, like she had doled out dribble cups instead. Neophytes fresh to New York, bright- eyed and thick-mouthed over cheap black coffee in blue and white Greek keyed cups wedged themselves into whatever spaces they could find, too afraid to ask for an ease up on the three spoons of synth sugar automatically thrown into each six ounce cup, feeling their fate pulse dully off the ones who had begun brewing coffee at four a.m. each morning just to avoid the entire ordeal.

Sunglasses balanced on the tips of every nose. The boat bounced on the waves, the orange paint of its safety railings clashing with the green lead paint coating its interior and the metallic white haze of sky drooping down around them.

Everything looked like it smelled worse than it actually did. It was like riding in a marketing ploy on behalf of the city itself to make the riders yearn for more, so that the arrival in the famed city that no longer stayed awake would factor in psyches as larger than the now crippled lives lived out within it.

Her mind reeled as she slid her feet back into her heels and wound the ribbons around her legs. The closer the boat got to South Ferry Terminal, the more lightheaded she became. She couldn't remember the last time she'd consumed anything other than alcohol and processed soy. Her knees buckled slightly as the first crowd of the day pushed its way out of the belly of the leviathan, ready to carry her out dead or alive.

The escalators creaked under the weight of the caffeine soaked morning crew as they re-adjusted themselves to the deluge of news that would be the topic of water-purifier conversation for the first part of the day. No notice was taken of her as she glided through the giant holo-screens that shouted national news onto the already weighed-down heads of the worker ants, stepping over hologram rats delivering personal @iM messages into the ankle receivers of the appropriate party. The juxtaposition of the new technology to the retro-active filth of the ferry used to move her. The area had been decimated in the last bombings, which had made it of no interest to the powers that held the economic reins of the gelded city.

After the Ferris wheel at Coney Island had toppled, the subsequent recapture of South Ferry by the few artists who still aimed for NYC and skateboard gypsies who treated its ruined coves as perfect stages for the futuristic freak show that bloomed wherever they did used to give Artyo hope that the New York she had once sought out as a refuge still had enough juice in it to revert to its true nature.

Oblivious to the pocket of space made around her made by the "Probably a Prostitute" looks shot in her direction for not being in any uniform recognizable to their homogenized minds, she strode up to the first bank of original lockers saved from the heap by the efforts of a band of petty drug dealers. They had lobbied to have them treated as some sort of defiantly historical landmark in order to keep their best stash spots in the city in place, and gotten so high off of making the system work for them that it had given many the balls to launch careers as true criminals in politics.

Crawling across the floor on her knees, upturned ass wiggling as if she was enjoying the sensation of the spectacle more than anyone who could have seen it, she gingerly pulled out the indigo-ink stained key that had been pressed into the top edge of her panties for safe-keeping, jamming it into the lock aggressively with the fleshy part of her left palm. The old lock clicked and her satchel fell out.

She slid back through the crowd to the click of her own heels and into the filthy public restroom the movie Desperately Seeking Susan had burned into her memory decades ago via incessant holo-runs on the wire.

Ignoring the throng of women preening in the stench of meth'd out piss, she reached down into her skirt to unsnap the crotch of her thong with one hand as she undid the hooks of the jacket pushing up her bosom with the other. Other women who'd come in to pull at hems or sniff spoons of powder up narrow noses glared at her as she partially undressed. After pulling the thong off and tossing it, she doused and dried herself to the disgust of mothers struggling with awestruck children who hadn't been able to hold it until they got to ADHD-approved daycare. Moms yanked little hands away from tiles that hadn't been sanitized in hours and dragged them out, indifferent to letting their kids see other career-oriented women start their days off coated in coke just like mommy, but running from what they prayed to gods of material things that their little darlings would not grow up to become, all that they saw housed in the half naked woman washing herself in the sink. In moments, all the stalls had emptied.

The oddly emancipated Bodhisattva stood staring at herself in the mirror as a scared smile spread across her face. She pulled a pair of pinking shears from her bag. In a few kamikaze snips of the scissors, she began to morph into the angel she was versus the avatar that she had never meant to be. Instincts in her that she'd worn down sharpened themselves against the blades of the pinking shears.

As the ritualistic self-tonsure of her locks played out, she consciously made her first entry into her body with no threat of fight or flight. Hair she had grown out over two thousand inhalations lay all over the sink she pressed her right thigh into for balance. As she cut jaggedly she thought of the Rastafarians dishonoring their locks, of Dominicans like Thyaz binding braids of hair that snaked to the middle of their backs, of nuns and monks shaving their heads and of Lenny Kravitz cutting off his locs. With each clip, a comment on her not being passive enough or too creative to be accepted dropped away. With each slice of the scissors hair with the ultimate intent of being all over the place balanced itself out.

Those who spiritually hounded her on his behalf and those who had fallen like trees unheard in forests were recalled by mirrors if no one else. Now on the other side both camps stood peering out at her.

The devaggressiva that she needed to be to make the final lunge waited for her in the forefront of the other side of the mirror with the progeny and already passed over snatches of herself at its back, all watching as her visuals in the world at-large caught up. Artyo stuck out her tongue and grinned at the giggly little girls and boys already in the world on other side of the mirror. She stepped out of the skirt into a pair of low-slung, de-fragmented jeans. Her skin seeped through areas of the fabric that were rubbed away like she had worn them while being dragged across asphalt repeatedly.

Aviators were shoved absently up onto the crown of her head. She pulled on a pair of old Onitsuka Tigers. The corset jacket was tossed and replaced with a stretchy white a-shirt that left nothing to the imagination. Still grinning like a fool, she sunk her teeth into her own lip, letting the thin sheen of her own blood stain her mouth before smearing them with more Lipglass. Slightly in order, Artyo headed out to the second set of lockers on the opposite edge of the terminal.

After making her way down the back row, she sat down, retrieved the appropriate key from her bag, and went thru the same slammed palm circumstance in order to leave as few prints as possible. The evidence spools that she had gone to pains to mass duplicate in the form of press kits tumbled into her lap. She checked the envelopes posted to various news agencies with explicit explanations of what they'd find in the lockers and shoved them into the satchel.

Hopping up into a crawl, she pulled a roll of quarters out of her bag and slinked along the floor sliding in coins, retrieving keys and tossing in a kit per locker as she went along.

At the end of the row she sat back down on the floor, pulled micro pore tape from the satchel and affixed a matching key to

each envelope, knowing the metal would set off the alarms upon entry into the designated systems, calling attention directly to them in the hair-trigger environment New York had become. She then dropped the envelopes at the various postboxes through the financial district she'd scouted out prior to the massacre.

The iron bull begged its final forehead kiss from her, the jagged grace of her bending down to do so in complete contrast to the skittish people scurrying around her. At the last mailbox across the street from the stock exchange, the concept of time re-registered to her. She hissed to no one in particular as she crumpled up the now empty paper bag, tossed it into the garbage can and was on her way to rip the last vestiges of herself free the only way she knew how.

chapter twenty seven

Back on the dais, The old queen of the closest to Heaven most beings had ever known was inconsolable, though those in attendance at court had no way of knowing. The children felled for speaking out against filial mandates continued at its relentless pace, and the lines between those being Punished and those in Puryf blurred between stasis states.

The only noticeable difference, one that quietly alarmed all courtesans present in a way they could not put their manicured fingertips on, was the absence of the spindle- haired one resting a palm in the old crone's lap. But the Empyrean aristocrats did what was expected of them. They collectively ignored the joy no longer flushing the cheeks of the old lady as child after child laid in spiritual heaps at her bare, rough feet for the sake of her amusement.

Puryf continued in the Per-a Complex of the Empyrean as usual until the one who held the Fate of all in her hands leapt up and yanked a particular child that reminded her of her daughter away from those who were trying to drown her, to the shock of all present, then smote the offending ones on the spot. The child looked up into the face of the old lady with the clearest blue eyes the old woman had seen in an eternity.

"Thank you-for saving me, after life." The child whispered.

The queen laughed gently, and a nervous titter slashed through the crowd as she mounted the dais and snapped her fingers. Beautiful towels were presented and she gingerly dried the shaking child in her lap. Martyrs began singing as the nobles picked up stones once more and pelted them while ANCs moved through the open space discarding bodies again.

When the old lady remembered that her daughter's eyes had been such a deep brown that they were almost black when not faded to all white, she shrieked.

"You- you're not her!" she screamed.
"Not who, my Savior-Queen?" the child asked timidly and started to cry again.

The old woman's eyes went black. The queen gnashed her teeth, wrapped her hands around the child's neck and strangled the imposter herself, in front of all, then leapt off the dais and violently held the child's head under water in the holy basin the queen had just saved her from until there was no longer an ounce of spirit in her. She roughly flung the spiritless body of the child over the heads of all the courtiers, from the throne all the way out over the precipice that the ANCs normally dumped the refused ones from.

All in attendance cowered from her as she howled, crumpling, forehead on the seat of her throne. Her head whirled around, causing every face her gaze landed on to burst into flames, all spontaneously combusting to ash except the flame-retardant ANCs, who went about business as usual sweeping ash over the precipice for eons, as nobles who moved up in the ranks gingerly pushed into the throne-room, indifferent to what had happened to the ones before them, ignoring rumors already circulating about the only true path towards what they all secretly strived for in the afterlife.

chapter twenty eight

Japan. Shibuya station. 10pm. Gigantic Panasonic screens suspended from skyscrapers and riveted to inner-city overpasses screamed about the hottest crazes and beamed the newest J-pop videos down onto the captive audience where all the streets bottomed out into the district's largest transit hub.

Thyaz pushed towards the station through the crowd at the bottom of Dogenzaka-dori. Past fourteen-year-old Japanese girls in school uniforms and stripper shoes they could not walk more than five steps at a time in. They flirted aggressively with the drunken salarimen as old as their absentee fathers who zigzagged towards the trains after carousing all night with their coworkers, jaggedly cut bangs streaked with multi-colored mascara, whispering that used panties they could buy in vending machines had nothing on the ones they'd worn all day. Teasing them with little "discoveries" like the colors painted in their hair for the evening just happened to match the briefs their moms had laid out for them earlier that morn.

He shoved past Israeli and Iranian ex-pats hawking homemade jewelry and fake phone cards to any patsy that got close enough to hit with their soft sell. Beautiful Gaijin girls of every nationality dashed past him with Venti-sized cups of Starbuck's coffee in order to grab that last train down into Roppongi to work at their respective hostess bars, sex clubs and piano lounges. Every foreigner that swooped past with any semblance of street-smarts in their exotic surroundings was optically devoured by the young Japanese kids who couldn't wait to get the hell out of Tokyo, and completely ignored by the ones who knew they'd never get a chance to.

His neck stiffened under the pressure of the square. No one gave a fuck that he had the shakes, but his inner animosity was easily overridden by his outer disgust with the people that swarmed him in the closest thing to a home that he had at this point. He rolled his eyes the way he always did when he needed to feel like he was over whoring himself amongst the insanities of Japan. Mid-roll, his eyes blinked in disbelief as Artyo's face was suddenly digitized before him. He closed his eyes, disoriented, breathing deeply for a few counts so that the hallucination would pass. He opened his eyes again and the last little bit of stomach he had gave way. It was no hallucination.

The images of Artyo flashed in a media blitz being pulsed across all ten of the giant televisions bolted to the sides of the buildings that shined down on the streets. Childlike voices of ten different newscasters sweetly pronounced the syllables of what ran across the bottom of their respective screens in roughly translated Hiragana.

"ABUSED CHILD-WOMAN SLAYS FAMILY-STILL AT LARGE-"

He looked down at his hands to see if he had just vaporized. The bony knuckles had gone white but were still there. The shakes dug into him full force and he began to sweat profusely.

"-Got a light?" He whispered hoarsely to no one in particular as he rammed a bent Gaulouise cigarette between his chapped lips. Taking a long drag, he pushed thru the crowd towards the turnstiles and stumbled onto the train to Shinjuku with the help of the padded cattle-prodders packing everyone in.

The movement of the train made him even greener as he fumbled to stay afloat, head and shoulders above most of the other travelers on the Yamanote line.

He felt worse when he closed his eyes. His hands were sticky with sweat and he smelled like fear to the majority of tipsy companions pressing their heads into his ribcage for support as the train sped through the curves. The Ka of Thyaz held on for dear life as it tore through the labor of manifesting what was to be somewhere else in the city.

For the first time in eight years, Thyaz got lost in the bowels of Shinjuku station for a good half an hour before getting claustrophobic and making a break for fresh air up any exit that might offer it. He was blocks away from the club he was headed to in the first place, the arms and legs of mean, drunk salarimen consciously tripping up the cagey Gaijin.

He arrived at Exodus in a bruised panic. The doorman who had watched his deterioration over the past few months the

way others rubberneck at train-wrecks was taken aback by the sheen to his face and the clarity in his eyes. Without a word, the gatekeeper in all white nodded to the Sumo-style bouncer in the badly cut gray suit and black Hanes tee, who ushered Thyaz to the private bathroom in the VIP section to clean himself up a bit before mingling with the guests.

Thyaz smiled weakly, shut the door behind him, and began to hurl as all that he'd taken during his descent began to hit at once.

"Likelgiveafuck-" he slurred aloud to his reflection as he wobbled over the chunks of rum-soaked fast food, bile, and splatters of blood in the sink.

"Likelgiveafuck-crazy ass-"

"They're gonna-" the Ka of Thyaz calmly began.

"

SHUT UP!!" He screamed and glared at his disheveled self in the mirror. "What the fuck do you care? - What the fuck is this night about, anyway? Us-? Or her?" he spat at the mirror image of himself.

His Ka climbed out the mirror to stand face to face with him. The Ka of Thyaz turned on the cold water and plugged the sink, humming to his flesh as he splashed his own face with it, smoothing his eyebrows, giving himself a smile. Spinning around violently, the soul of Thyaz grabbed himself by his filthy ponytail and slammed Thyaz's face into the basin full of water as he struggled against himself. The Ka of Thyaz checked himself out in the mirror as he drowned his personality and narrowed his eyes as warnings about spiritual fouls began to go off in the background of his mind.

"Itstoolateforallthissentimentalshit-" The Ka of Thyaz whispered, yanking a gray Thyaz back up from the depths. He shoved him against the wall and slicked the front part of Thyaz's hair back with water the way a mom fixes a cowlick with spit before crossing the threshold into church.

"Itstoolateforallthissentimentalshit- we can't change it-"

Thyaz's soul snarled. "She isn't thinking about you! -She can't even hear you anymore-fuck her!!But there is no way she's getting out before we do-Now ... we're going to take a recalibrating piss, snort some shit, down a few drinks, finally get you shit-faced-so I can end this nightmare tonight-fuck her -Fuckher!! " he screamed and then smiled softly at himself, seeing the comedy in his own melodrama without her there to quietly point it out.

"...Wonder what the fuck her crazy ass did-" Thyaz whispered as he drained himself from the three days before this one spent trying to drink on the courage to do what his only out was. Thyaz started to laugh as he pictured her jumping out of trees onto their backs, or breaking into houses and cars, knocking them off one at a time, ninja- style. By the time he stepped back into himself and left the bathroom, he was giddy. Manhattan in hand and out on the floor, he squeezed himself between two speakers and leaned his head into the vibrations of bass ripping through the one on his left.

He closed his eyes and tried to have the imagery of her washed away by the pain of the noise. His eyes popped open as the opening riffs of the remix of "Invincible" PROPHET did for Artyo got spliced into the action. The last blood in Thyaz's head drained out of his face as images of Artyo were thrown up on the gigantic video screens built into the floor, walls and ceiling of the place.

He sat pinned to the wall as he watched a play by play of what was going down stateside on her behalf, floored by the vividness of it all. On the dance floor, Artyo Jaymes was being canonized- as the brave new world's legend of Billie Jean with her gang of uprising cousins- for offing the adults that tried to systematically destroy the kids they brought into the world.

Cheers of "Gambatte" erupted in waves. "How the hell do they have this footage here?" he screeched as the truth of it slapped him in the face.

"Because she knew you'd stumble in here soon enough to hide - she's the one who blitzed it to the new agencies- she's the one who forwarded it all to the-she's lost her damn-" Thyaz shuddered and bit down on his lip so hard that he cut it.

The taste of old broken cigarettes made him even more nauseous as it mingled with the blood. Then everything shifted into slow motion. Sitting still, the room seemed to spin around him.

On the packed dance floor, his eyes kept being drawn up to the racks of the lighting system. Everything Thyaz had called himself a liar for seeing over the years flashed in front of his eyes. The longer he stared, the clearer the guardian angels became who floated over the dance floor.

They looked down at their charges, the partying club-kids. Manufactured smiles forcibly smashed into their stony faces. The smiles wouldn't let him tear his eyes away- sweet, sticky. Thinly veiled malevolence. It was only then that he started to see all the strings descending down into the crowd. Marionette strings twisting the various posers interspersed between the club kids to and fro. For each step a charge made towards a kid with similar light, a tug of the strings above pulled some ashen-faced poser into his or her path.

The guardian angels tangled their own charges up in knots of past thoughts and planted memories of people in efforts not to have them synch up with any energy that might advance them out of the stage of being charged to an Angelic host.

The assigned angels at work snarled at the guardians more lax about the potential couplings, and shoved all sorts of emotional infidels into the mix in hopes of a fight or two breaking out to keep their assigned slates blank enough to keep the entities Empyrean-employed and down on earth.

The guardians felt comprehending energy absorbing their covert actions openly from somewhere in the crowd.

Ousted by this energy pulsing where there had not been any before, a smoke-machine wraith spun around as if ready to smote Thyaz as he blandly looked away from what Artyo came into his life pointing out as real.

The fear of indifference suddenly coated the wraith and quickly spread to the twisted hosts alongside it like an airborne infection. The Geppetto Guardian angels collectively fell into a state of screeching shock before they spontaneously combusted into shards of light over the dance floor. The club kids cheered at the latest pyrotechnics they thought they were tripping out to. Thyaz downed his drink.

"They're going to kill you Mahmi-" He whispered to the Heart of himself 8000 miles away.

"Only if I don't beat them to it-" He heard her whisper back before she blocked his signal again.

The surprise of hearing her voice in his head again after craving it for so long caused him to spit some of his amped up Manhattan into his lap. The thought that followed, that she had been listening in on him all along made him roar with rage. Pissed, Thyaz jumped up and pushed through the crowd in search of release from the pressure around his solar plexus. Underground Angels cried out like banshees at his gleaming visage and shoved their offspring out of his way as if he and what was overriding him were contagious. His legs shot out from under him as if the Devil himself was on his tail, but it was anger and hurt that pushed him onward, not fear of anything else other than that she had finally stopped loving him.

He stopped running when his legs threatened to collapse beneath him. He glowed as if he were radioactive. The heavy air of Tokyo at night had him gasping. His eyes were sticky from hot tears, sweat and rage erupting out of him in the middle of rainy season in Japan.

The bursts of drunken English at ear-level set him straight before full-on vertigo hit, and he suddenly became aware that he had ran all the way from Shinjuku down to Roppongi and was heaving for air under the overpass intro to the High-Touch town he had slowly died in over almost twelve years.
He shoved past the slimy guys trolling for tourists to coax into hostess clubs out in front of Almonds' pink and white canopy and headed down the street that made Roppongi crossing what it was. Catcalls from regulars who wanted to be known for knowing him chased him down deeper into a head that was full of enraged screams.

"Thigh-baby!" A familiar voice called out to him as a sinewy shoulder came out of nowhere and blocked his path. It was Spaniel, his ex-roommate, with two demon-like yakuza thugs flanking him like shiny sharkskin wings.

"Man- look at you-" Spaniel slurred, the alcohol in his portly system and the bodyguards making his closeted middle Minnesota ass flame like Halley's comet in a clear midnight sky. "It's been so long since we've- Hey roomy-" he slobbered and laughed to himself as his left hand went up to play with the stream of spit that had escaped.

Thyaz recoiled, as if he had almost stepped in feces. He was pulled out of his downward spiral long enough to wonder what the fuck Spaniel was smoked out on. Spaniel laughed aloud and spat next to the shoe of one of the thugs.

"You always were quite the dramatic byshunfu, Thyaz!" Spaniel snorted. "I always had to remind myself you weren't just a big, beautiful girl down on her luck when you'd be sleeping with your back to me on the floor of my-" he stopped himself as if he'd lost the words he needed to move forward.

Thyaz rolled his eyes and went to push past him. The arm of the giant Japanese guy to his left sprung up to block him again. The huge grunt raised a slashed brow above partially reflective sunglasses that captured a grayish yet calm Ka of Thyaz with the lights of a late-night Tokyo fanned out behind his head.

The thug sported a military buzz-cut with a wisp of hair at the nape of his neck, the tips of which had been bleached blond. The cheap sharkskin pants the muscle wore matched the jacket he held in his other hand. He had the sleeves of his translucent black striped shirt rolled up, exposing the multi-colored tattoo of a black-faced Biggie Smalls, "Rest in Peace" woven into the flowers and vines that wound themselves around the rest of the forearm. The ink of the tattoos spread across his torso stood out against his turmeric- toned skin through the transparent top.

Spaniel laughed and spun around to look up at the stony faces of his henchmen with pride of purchase. "I still do not get it- I saw the dick- it wasn't that "impressive" if you know what Ah mean, but you did have the balls to-"

"What the fuck do you want?" Thyaz barked, adrenaline coursing through him in reaction to how horrible he and his soul looked pulled together in the lenses of the muscle's glasses more than due to anything Spaniel said.

"Oh yeah, your bitch is all over the news-or the meant to be your bitch but wasn't -" Spaniel snarled nastily.

"I knew just by your response when I asked for her panties on the phone in front of your face-"

The Ka of Thyaz cut Spaniel off by grabbing him by the throat, growling. The color came back into Thyaz as it drained out of Spaniel dangling a foot above the ground. The two roughnecks stepped back in surprise. Reflective shoved up his shades and held back his lace-shirted, glen plaid suited, longhaired buddy from jumping before given the signal by Spaniel.

"If either one of these slow-mo fucks you hired even blinks, I will rip your fucking thyroid out, you repressed son of a bitch." the Ka of Thyaz glowered through Thyaz's flesh.

Spaniel wheezed. "Why is it always the mention of the panty thing that gets you? It's not like you- you know- fucked her or anything-" He gasped.

"-Shut the fuck up-" the Ka of Thyaz snarled through Thyaz's lips.

"I just don't get that-" Spaniel whimpered on. "You said so yourself-"

Thyaz's grip tightened on Spaniel's neck. "You need to get "shut the fuck up-" He growled.

Spaniel's face began to turn blue, a first for either wannabe Yakuza-boy to witness. The thought of stopping Thyaz was defeated by the childlike curiosity that came with watching a Gaijin get strangled to death in front of a street full of Japanese folks.

Spaniel made whiny wheezing sounds and flimsy grasps at Thyaz's hands as he kicked his tiny feet aimlessly.

Then he saw the sky go red due to a blood vessel rupturing inside one of his eyes. Suddenly, Artyo's laugh erupted in Thyaz's head and brought him back into the moment and the strangling he was in the midst of doing.

He rolled his eyes and slammed his inner hands over his inner ears in protest. "...This is pointless!" he muttered, dropped Spaniel in the gutter and walked off, shoving past the Yakuza boys and ducking down a narrow, foreigner- filled block.

Spaniel wheezed back to normality, put on his own sunglasses at night and walked off in the opposite direction, shameful at having lost the little face he'd had with his hired help. The Yakuza boys silently fell in behind him.

Thyaz settled into the Brink, a dingy gaijin bar tucked back in the cut. He watched the coverage as he tried once again to drown his soul in whatever was on tap. Other Gaijins milled around him, recalling the killing-spree face on the screen as his old kind of/sort of business partner, terrified to ask any questions of the burnt-out hustler who'd been publicly dervishing in his own floating world death dance for the past year.

The end.

ABOUT THE AUTHOR

Author and multimedia artist Angel Brynner has marched to the beat of her
own drum across the arts for over two decades. After formal training with
the vanguard of the menswear industry she helmed her own line of men's
clothing and produced events for the collection in the club scenes of
New York and Tokyo.

She became quietly known for the futuristic cautionary tales back-dropping
her collections, taking over clubs and the guerilla-marketing style she used
to slam her vision into the hearts of her fans. While being sponsored by
Multinational companies desiring audience with her underground tribe, she
returned from Japan to her hometown to press charges against a pedophile
before the statute of limitations ran out.

Cast as a vigilante by a corrupt sex crimes unit for trying to protect another
child from the same attacker, during the media onslaught against
the first brave adults to come forward and press charges against
the Catholic priests that had abused them as children she was hit with a
vision of all those already lost in a sick war on kids no one talked about.

She committed herself & her art to doing something about it.

The grievechronic universe was forged in the fires of imagining the
Armageddon that would erupt through a generation of kids who
had finally had enough abuse at the hands of adults and
banded together under their grievances.
The epic spiritual, metaphysical, and historical implications
of such an event played out on every level- from the hellish norms
that caused it to what would be called heaven by such a broken world-
made her head spin.

Published by Kokopellima Press, each free-standing installment of grievechronic
Is a take-no- prisoners tale.

Alongside AOLAB[the active-art series featuring the multimedia work
that fed Eutaxis, Ecclesia, Exodus, Erebus, Exist and the kinetic collection
of novels that follow them], Angel Brynner's books are the culmination of
an artistic journey many years in the making,
all leading to a mysterious future project entitled **Transcendence.**

The first THREE books of the /grievechronic\ series

EUTAXIS ECCLESIA EXODUS

Are now exclusively Available in audiobook form

@ elevenreader.io

Books   Series

Eutaxis. /Grievechronic\ book one.

Angel Brynner

EXODUS. /grievechronic\ book three.

Angel BRYNNER

ECCLESIA. /grievechronic\ book two.

Angel BRYNNER

Eutaxis. /Grievechronic\ book one.

Angel Brynner

EXODUS. /grievechronic\ book three.

Angel BRYNNER

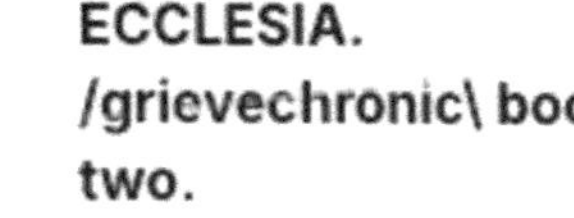

ECCLESIA. /grievechronic\ book two.

Angel BRYNNER

False utopias look like heaven when they exist inside of you, but the spell breaks when you fall. Halcyon days harbor great space for healing if they can stand being held up to the light. The memories we run and hide in may overlap or coincide, but underneath each pleasing space is all that we have yet to face. Hiding bodies to embrace the good is par for the course. But those bones must live again in order to truly break free. The good goes down in spite of what you have to ignore to be grateful for it, but ignoring shit doesn't make anything really go away….and going away only goes so far.

"It looks like Heaven." That may be true. But don't forget what you've gone through

Elysum
before or after the fall may never have been Paradise at all.

ISBN 978-1-950077-83-0

9 781950 077830

52000

Coming in 2024
Angel Brynner
ELYSIUM
/grievechronic\

www.ingramcontent.com/pod-product-compliance
Lightning Source LLC
Chambersburg PA
CBHW040534170726
48295CB00012B/463